SUMMER SANCTUARY

LAURIE GRAY

LUMINIS BOOKS
Published by Luminis Books
13245 Blacktern Way, Carmel, Indiana, 46033, U.S.A.
Copyright © Socratic Parenting, LLC, 2010

Cover image photographed and created by Kenneth Harkenrider.
Cover design and composition for *Summer Sanctuary* by Joanne Riske.

Grateful acknowledgment is made to Harper & Row Publishers, Inc.,
for permission to adapt the last two sentences from *Charlotte's Web* for
the author's dedication. Copyright © 1952 by E. B. White. All rights
reserved.

Genesis 34: 1–2 is quoted from *The Holy Bible, New International
Version.* Copyright © 1978 by New York International Bible Society.

ISBN-10: 1-935462-34-2

ISBN-13: 978-1-935462-34-7

Printed in the United States of America

10 9 8 7 6 5 4 3 2 1

Early Praise for *Summer Sanctuary:*

What a big-hearted story, told with affection and humor. I loved spending time with Matthew and his family and with Dinah, the girl who looks in from outside. Like Dinah, young readers will find a place of welcome and comfort, a true sanctuary, in the pages of this book. Like Matthew, they'll discover something important about friendship and independence.

—*Helen Frost*, *Printz Honor Award-winning author of* *Keesha's House*

Summer Sanctuary exudes a strong voice for the two central characters . . . they learn what it means to measure a person's worth not based on circumstances, but on the will to survive. Gray has captured the essence of what it means to be a young teen—wanting to grow as an individual while needing the security of a home and loving family. *Summer Sanctuary* can help guide teens through the difficult transition between childhood and becoming adults.

—*Kayleen Reusser*, *author of* *Taylor Swift—A Blue Banner Biography*

Go to www.luminisbooks.com to find discussion questions for *Summer Sanctuary*.

The author is deeply grateful to the following people for their advice, encouragement and support:

Marcia Amidon Lüsted for her excellent instruction and editing.

For their thoughtful reading of the first draft, many thanks to Beth Schleisman, Nikki Busenbark, Peggy Virgil, Deb Sanchez, Bonnie Lloyd, Maria Camacho, Jon DeDee, and Teresa Landis.

Andrea Landis and DeAnna Barnes, my first teen readers.

Helen Frost, Kayleen Reusser, and my Fort Wayne SCBWI critique group.

Tracy Richardson and Chris Katsaropoulos of Luminis Books.

To Victoria, my unexpected miracle and muse.

To Frank, for keeping me warm and safe and dry while I write.

For Robin,

It is not often that someone comes along who is a true friend and a good writer. Robin was both.

❧ One ❧

THE FIRST TIME I saw Dinah, I thought she was a boy. Now that the summer's almost over, it's hard to believe that guy in jean shorts, dirty-white jogging shoes, and an oversized black t-shirt was even her. I was sitting on a bench in front of the library. I saw this guy sprawled out on the grass off to the side, soaking up the warm June sun. He had a newspaper spread out around him, but I had the funny feeling he was watching me as I choked down half of the turkey and Swiss sandwich my mom made me. Turkey and Swiss is my favorite, only I like it with mayonnaise. Mom made this one with mustard. Yuck.

I washed the mustard down with water from my sports bottle. Mom always chose mustard over mayonnaise in the summertime, like the mayonnaise would spoil the second I stepped out of the house. I examined the remaining sandwich half. The mustard had soaked into both slices of bread. It was smeared all over the turkey and all over the cheese. No getting around it. I put it back in the sandwich bag and tossed it in the trash.

At that moment I was convinced the whole summer was going to suck—only I'm not allowed to say "suck." My best friend Kyle left the week before to spend two months with his grandparents on a farm a hundred miles away. Kyle's the kind of guy every kid likes. I'm the kind of guy every kid's mom likes. And speaking of moms, my mom was pregnant. AGAIN. So the chances of me getting my own room before I'm 20 were now absolutely zero. Zip.

I've wanted my own room forever. Kyle has his own room. I share my room with my next-youngest brother, Mark. I'm older, but Mark hit a growing spurt last winter. He was already as big as I was and destined to pass me this summer. Then he plastered posters of all his soccer and baseball heroes all over his side of the room this past spring. It was like a daily reminder of everything I'd never be.

I realized the guy was still watching me. His eyes followed me as I walked into the library. He was acting so creepy for a guy. It was giving me the willies. I mean, I'd never had a guy watch me like that. My heart pounded, and the mustard in my stomach churned. One time I heard my grandfather preach about guys who like guys instead of girls. He called it the "abomination of reprobates." I shuddered; Grandpa's most booming preacher voice echoed the word *re-pro-bate-suh* in my head. When Grandpa thunders from the pulpit, you half-expect God to throw down a bolt of lightning for good measure. Everyone in the whole congregation prays he isn't the biggest sinner there.

My dad's a preacher, too. When I asked him about the abomination of reprobates, he gave me a little book called *Reprobation Asserted* by John Bunyan. Now, I liked John Bunyan's book *Pilgrim's Progress*, which was kind of like a Christian adventure novel. His reprobation book read more like a really, really long sermon. Somewhere in Chapter Two I read that "reprobate" means "void of judgment." I gave the book back to Dad. Kyle's the one who finally told me what Grandpa was talking about.

Inside the library, I went straight to the front window and watched the reprobate through the dark glass. Why did he pick me to watch anyway? Definitely weird. Something was up. He looked all around before he carefully folded up the newspaper and very deliberately stuffed it deep inside the trash can. There was something peculiar about the way he did it, but I couldn't quite put my finger on it. Then he walked over to the same bench where I'd been sitting, and I saw what he had in his hand. My sandwich!

He sat down on the bench and crossed his legs like a girl. I watched him put the sandwich right up to his nose and smell it. Then he opened it up, pulling the mustard-glued turkey from one piece of bread, the mustard-glued cheese from the other. After a thorough examination, he reassembled the sandwich and took a small bite. He chewed so slowly, like he was savoring every drop of mustard. I about gagged just watching him.

But the more I watched him, the more something told me it wasn't a guy. By the time he was done with the sandwich, I was pretty sure he was a she and not some weirdo. Well, it was still weird. And I had a million questions: Who was she? How hungry would you have to be to eat trash? How could you be that hungry and eat so slowly?

She ate every crumb. She even licked the mustard and crumbs from the plastic bag. Then she stuffed the bag in the front pocket of a tattered black backpack. I couldn't take my eyes off of her. I willed her to come into the library so I could get a closer look.

When she did, I nearly tripped over myself dashing to the nearest bookshelf. I grabbed the first book I reached and stuck my nose in it. After she passed by I realized I had buried myself in a quilting book. *What a loser!* I groaned as I put the book back on the shelf.

She walked behind me over to the tables by the magazines. She pulled two chairs out from under a table and turned them to face each other. Then she pulled a spiral notebook and pen out of the overstuffed backpack. She sat in one chair with her backpack and feet on the other. She chewed on the pen as she flipped through the notebook.

I wanted to talk to her so badly. Just the thought made my palms sweaty. I didn't exactly have much experience talking to girls, only Kyle's sister, Amanda. And she mostly just ignored us. I guessed this girl was about the same age as Amanda—fourteen, maybe fifteen. It was hard to tell. I concentrated on breathing deeply as I meandered toward her.

I picked up a *National Geographic* magazine off the rack and sat down at the table behind her. I studied her profile. She was kind of pretty; funny ears, though.

Then again, maybe everybody's ears are funny, and I just never noticed. Her light brown hair was neatly trimmed around her ear, but all chopped up in the back. Like she'd turned her back on a mad barber, and just barely escaped with her life.

When she caught me staring at her, I hid my face behind the magazine. She tossed her notebook and pen on the table. When I looked at her again, her blue eyes burned right through me, catching my ears on fire.

"What?" She shot the word right at me, her head recoiling from the force.

I turned my head around and looked from side to side. I raised my eyebrows and gave her my most innocent and surprised look. "I'm sorry," I said. "Are you talking to me?"

She narrowed her eyes. "What are you looking at?" she demanded.

Our eyes remained locked. I held up the magazine. "*National Geographic*," I croaked. There was a long, awkward silence, but neither of us blinked. I cleared my throat. Then I mustered up every ounce of courage I possessed and blurted out, "What's your name?"

She squinted her eyes at me again. "Who wants to know?"

"I do," I said, doing my best impersonation of my dad's voice.

"And who are you?" She took her feet off the chair and turned slightly toward me in her chair.

"My name is Matthew." I stood up and offered her my hand like a man. "What's your name?" I asked again.

This time she ignored my question and my hand. "How old are you, Matthew?" she asked.

I felt my shoulders and back straighten as I replied, "Almost thirteen."

"So you're twelve." She waited for me to agree. I sat back down instead. "What grade are you in, Matthew?"

I hated that question. Everybody thinks that's like the easiest question in the world—only I can explain Pythagoras' theorem in less time than I can answer that question. And Pythagoras is more interesting. I wanted her to think I was cool, so I tried to be mysterious. "I'm not in a grade," I said, crossing my arms.

"Yeah, right," she replied. "It's summer vacation. Nobody's in a grade. What grade will you be in when school starts up again?"

"It depends," I said. I shrugged my shoulders for effect.

"Depends on what?" she asked, draping her arms over the chair across from me. "On whether or not you flunked?"

The word flunked was like a slap in the face. "I've never flunked," I countered, forgetting to be cool. "My family home schools. I'm at a different grade level for every subject." I waited for her to laugh or make fun of me, but she didn't.

"Really?" she said with a serious frown. "So what's your highest grade level?"

"I'm at a twelfth grade reading level," I replied evenly.

"What's your lowest grade level?"

"I don't know. I'm doing sophomore level math and science. Probably social studies is my lowest. I'm just starting high school work in that."

She seemed genuinely interested all of a sudden. "So do you get a summer vacation when you're home schooled?"

"Not really . . . well, kind of, I guess. My mom only brings us to the library once a week during the school year. My deal with my parents this summer is I can study independently. I get to choose the project, and I can ride my bike to the library every day if I want.

Once I get my chores and stuff done, I mean. Every day except Sunday on account of church, and the library is closed." I was talking way too much. I still didn't even know her name or anything about her, except that she wasn't anything like any of the girls from my church.

"So how many brothers and sisters do you have?" She had moved to my table now, dragging her backpack with her.

"I have three younger brothers." I paused. "And another one on the way."

"Wow!" she exclaimed, raising both her eyebrows.

I tried to change the subject from me to her. "I've never seen you here before. Are you new in town?"

"Not exactly," she said. "I just discovered this branch of the library. I think I like it. So maybe I'll see you around. I gotta go now, though."

I thought I saw her smile as she slung her backpack over her shoulder and disappeared out the door.

ଔ TWO ଔ

AT DINNER THAT night I kept thinking about her. What was her name? She didn't look like an Amber or Melissa or Mary or Elizabeth or any other name I could think of. I was so startled when I heard Dad say *my* name that I dropped my fork.

"So, Matthew, what have you decided to study this summer?" Dad asked. I saw him look at my mom and raise his eyebrows. Mom shook her head.

"Earth to Matthew!" Mark shouted.

"Earth to Matthew," Luke echoed.

"Mattie, Mattie," Johnny mimicked.

"Boys," Mom scolded as she cut up Johnny's spaghetti and meatballs. "Let your brother answer."

"Einstein's Theory of Relativity and the speed of light," I said. "You know. Math and science stuff."

"Sounds very interesting. How about you, Mark?" Dad asked.

Mark slurped in the two long strands of spaghetti hanging out of his mouth. "Statistics and averages," Mark said as he chewed. What Mark really meant was that he was going to play baseball all summer. He was the youngest player in the 10-12 league, but already better than most of the guys my age. Way better than me. When he moved up into my league, I decided to hang up my cleats. Well, actually, I just gave them to Mark, since his feet were as big as mine already. Anyway, I mostly played just because Kyle did.

That night after my brothers were all asleep, I heard my mom and dad talking downstairs. I sneaked down and sat in the dark on the bottom step to hear what they were talking about. I'd been doing it for years. That's how I learned that Mom was the Tooth Fairy, that Dad wanted me to be a preacher just like him, and that Mom was going to have another baby.

That was all old news, except the preacher part. It seems like preachers have to take everything on faith. My dad has mountains of faith. So does my grandpa. Not me. I'm still working my way up to the mustard seed level. I like science with all its experiments and math with all its proofs. I just don't get how people can be so sure about things they can't prove. But I haven't told Dad that. Yet.

"Just how much money did she offer to donate?" I heard my mother asking.

"She offered as much as we need to complete the new youth center, even if we exceed the projected budget," my dad replied. "Up to a million dollars."

Mom whistled softly. "Well, that's certainly a generous offer—especially coming from a woman who never had any children of her own."

Who has lots of money and no children? My mind was racing through our congregation.

"It would be generous if there were no strings attached," Dad said.

"So what does she want?"

"You're not going to believe it." I peeked around the corner and saw my dad shaking his head as he sat by my mom on the couch. "She wants to be able to bring her dogs to church."

My mom laughed so loud, I nearly jumped out of my jammies. "All of them?" she howled. I retreated back a few steps, safely out of view.

"Really, Theresa, it's not funny." When Mom tried to stop laughing, she started hooting like an owl. "And, no, she doesn't want to bring all of them." Dad took a deep breath. "She'd like to bring two dogs to each service. She said that if she were blind I'd have to let her bring a seeing-eye dog, and that if she could have one of her dogs on each side of her as she listened to my sermons, she'd be much more capable of seeing and hearing the truth."

It must be old Mrs. Miller. Kyle and I once overheard his dad saying that she had more money than God and not a blessed idea what to do with any of it. She's got half a dozen fancy dogs that she paid tons of money for plus more strays than anyone's been able to count.

"So, you get your Promised Land, only it's already going to the dogs!" Mom was still laughing.

Dad sighed. "Right. The Israelites got the Land of Canaan, and I get the Land of Canine."

They stopped talking. I guessed they were kissing. Time for me to go back to bed.

❧ Three ❧

THE NEXT DAY, I couldn't get to the library soon enough. It opened at 10:00, and I watched Mrs. Cleary unlock the front doors. Mrs. Cleary had worked at the library since before I was born. She still wore her hair in one of those bouffant hairdos. The week before she ordered a bunch of books on relativity for me through interlibrary loan. She stood a little too close beside me and leaned over my shoulder to see my list. She smelled a little too much like the cafeteria at the Senior Center where we went Christmas caroling every year.

I planted myself on the bench outside the library and thought about the girl. I decided that her parents must be dead. Whoever she lived with must be so terrible that she had to run away. As I sat in front of the library that morning, though, our library didn't seem like a place for runaways. So I started thinking maybe she was mental. I read something once about people who are so crazy they eat dirt. They can't help it. They see dirt in a flowerbed or garden, and they just have to pick up a handful and shove it in their mouths. Maybe there's something like that with garbage. I'd have to research *that* if she didn't show up.

I almost forgot—it was Saturday. What if she couldn't come back until Monday? What if she didn't come back at all? Was she sneaking food out of other trash cans? Did she think I was a total loser—a short, skinny, freckle-faced nobody who liked to quilt? She left awful suddenly. Still—she did smile before she left. Not just a polite smile to dismiss me. It was a real smile that covered her whole face and included her eyes. *She'll be here. I just have to wait.*

I reached in my backpack and pulled out *The Last Battle*. Even though *The Chronicles of Narnia* series was my favorite, I couldn't concentrate. I never even turned a page. It was nearly 11:00 when I finally caught a glimpse of her approaching from the side. I didn't look up from the book until she was standing almost directly in front of me. She was wearing the same clothes as yesterday—same black t-shirt, same jean shorts, same scuffed-up white jogging shoes. When our eyes met, I said, "Oh, hi." I hoped she couldn't hear my heart pounding.

"Hi, Matthew," she replied. She sat down on the bench beside me, but not too close. I waited. Today she was going to have to do more of the talking.

"So," she said, looking me up and down, "you must have gotten all of your chores done early."

"Yeah. You were sure in a hurry yesterday. Everything okay?" I asked.

"Sure." She slipped her backpack off her shoulder and let it drop to the bench. It was every bit as full as it was yesterday, maybe even packed fuller. "I just had someplace else I had to be." Then she turned toward me, kind of hiding the backpack behind her.

"What about today? Is there someplace else you have to go?"

"Maybe," she replied. "What about you?"

"I don't have to be home until 3:00." There was an awkward pause. "Do you want to share my lunch with me?"

"Maybe. What's for lunch?" she asked.

"Let's see what my mom packed today," I said, rummaging through my backpack and pulling out a brown bag. I peered inside. "How do you feel about half a peanut butter sandwich, half a banana, and some pretzels?"

16

"I'd like that," she said. "But let's not eat it here. Let's have a picnic by the trees behind the library." She was on her feet instantly. "Come on."

I'd never had lunch with a girl before. I liked the idea of a picnic where no one could see us. I mean, what if Mom or Dad drove by? Or someone from the church? They'd want to know who she was. I wouldn't know what to tell them. Not that I was doing anything wrong. I got the feeling she really didn't want to be seen, either.

"How about right here?" she asked, settling in under the shade of a large maple tree.

"Okay," I said. There were lots of reddish-brown propellers all over the place—little helicopters to carry the maple seeds away in the wind. I plopped myself down right on top of them, Indian style. I'd never been back there before. I wasn't really sure if we were supposed to be there, but at least there was nobody else around. "So are you ever going to tell me your name?" I ventured.

"That all depends," she said very matter-of-factly. "Have you told anyone about me or asked anybody else anything about me?"

"No," I answered. I was relieved that I hadn't. I wanted to solve this mystery on my own. *Would I have told Kyle if he were here?*

"That's good," she said. "If you tell anyone about me, I'll be gone. You'll never see me again."

Somehow I could tell she wasn't kidding. "Well, I won't tell anyone then," I offered.

She stared at me a long time. I felt my palms getting sticky again. I wiped them on my khaki shorts. "Okay," she said finally. "I think I believe you, Matthew. My name is Dinah."

"Dinah," I whispered under my breath. The name danced around and lingered in my mouth like the bubbles from an ice-cold Mountain Dew. "Are you hungry, Dinah?" I asked. I knew she was. I knew that's how I got her back here all to myself. But what did I really know about hunger? I knew if she weren't hungry, she never would have noticed me, let alone told me her name.

"Sure. Let's eat." She pulled a beat-up water bottle out of her backpack and chugged down half of it while I divided up my lunch.

"It's creamy peanut butter," I advised her. "Some people only like crunchy."

"And some people are allergic to peanuts," she teased. "I like creamy best," she assured me.

"Me, too," I nodded, except I didn't. I liked crunchy. But there was never any crunchy peanut butter at our house because Johnny was still too young for crunchy. And by the time he was old enough, the new baby would be too young.

We ate in silence. I looked around, trying not to gawk at her while she ate. The wind gently swayed the tree limbs overhead. Little rays of sunshine slipped through the stirring leaves, sparkling on Dinah's face and hair. A robin hopping around at a safe distance behind us stopped and cocked its head at me. It quickly lost interest and flew away. I didn't care about the robin, but I didn't want Dinah to fly away again like yesterday.

Dinah broke the silence. "Why are you being so nice to me?" she asked. She was combing her fingers through the grass and propellers, watching intently as the blades bounced right back up, twirling the propellers in the air.

I didn't know what to say. I couldn't very well tell her that I watched her dig my sandwich out of the trash yesterday, and I was just dying of curiosity.

"You just seem different—more interesting than most of the people I see around here." I leaned back on my elbows and stretched my feet out in front of me. "Why did you agree to have lunch with me?"

"I was hungry," she said simply, rising to her feet and wiping her hands on the back of her jean shorts. She walked around the maple tree, hugging it with one arm as she walked. Then she turned around and walked the other way, hugging the tree with her other arm. She stopped right in front of me. I had to look straight up to see her face. "You seem different, too," she admitted. "In a good way." She sat down and relaxed a little, leaning back against the tree.

"Can you keep a secret?" she asked.

I hesitated. How many times had my parents talked to me about good secrets and bad secrets? Could I promise to keep a secret without knowing what kind of a secret it was? "I can keep a secret that needs to be kept."

"I mean it, Matthew." She sat forward, hugging her knees. "If I tell you something, you have to promise not to tell anyone." Just the way she said it I could tell it was a really serious secret.

"I promise," I said, knowing that I would keep Dinah's secret no matter what and hoping I wouldn't regret it.

❧ Four ❧

"LET'S WALK," DINAH said, and she was on her feet instantly. We picked up our backpacks and headed into the small woods. "I really didn't have any place to go yesterday," she confessed. "And I really don't have any place to go today. The truth is, I don't have any place to go for the next 20 days."

"What do you mean?" I asked.

"I mean I spent the last few nights in the playhouse at the park by the Y. Before that I spent a night in a barn out in the country. Only one, though." She paused, and I waited. "You wouldn't believe how loud cows can fart!" She put her lips to her arm and blew as hard as she could. I burst out laughing; then I tried it, too. "That's it!" Dinah screeched. "You sound exactly like a farting cow!" I couldn't wait to show Kyle my new talent. He probably spent all summer listening to cows fart.

"So where are your parents?" I asked between farts.

"I don't have a dad," she said blowing the biggest fart yet. "And my mom won't be back until July 9." She turned to look at me. I saw tears hiding behind her blue eyes. She tossed her head back and picked up the pace. I hustled to stay beside her.

"Isn't there anybody you can stay with?" Surely every kid had *somebody* who would take him in. "What about grandparents?"

"Nope. My mom grew up in about a dozen foster homes up in Michigan. No grandparents, aunts or uncles that I know of." We came to a small creek. At first I thought Dinah was going to wade right through it, but she turned abruptly to her left and walked along the edge, leaving me behind her. I caught a glimpse of my reflection shimmering in the water before I ran to catch up with her again. This time I kept her between myself and the creek.

"You don't have anybody at all?" I couldn't imagine a world without my parents. Or my brothers, either, which kind of surprised me.

"I have my mom, and she has me!" Dinah protested, dropping her backpack and grabbing the lowest branch of a sturdy oak. In what seemed like a single, smooth motion, she was suddenly perched above me. "I'm just on my own for the next couple of weeks."

I decided to climb the branch facing Dinah. It was a little bit higher, so I had to jump to reach it and scale the tree trunk until I was hanging upside down like a three-toed sloth. I struggled to right myself and felt the bark scraping away at the skin inside my legs. I gazed through the unfamiliar forest of trees around me until I caught a glimpse of a bridge over the creek that I recognized as part of the bike trails through our neighborhood.

Dinah leaned her back into the trunk of the tree and wrapped her arms around the branch above her. "What about your house?" I asked her. "Don't you have a house or apartment or someplace where you and your mom were living?"

"We were living with my mom's boyfriend," Dinah said. "But I'm not staying there without my mom."

"Why not?" I studied her shoes as they swung back and forth beneath the branch. They were laced up real tight, like maybe they were too big. I wondered if they were her mom's.

"Jerry's creepy," Dinah replied.

"Creepy like how?" I couldn't imagine my mom liking someone creepy.

"Like, we live in a one bedroom apartment, so I always sleep on the couch," Dinah said. "The very first night after my mom left, Jerry told me I should come sleep in the bedroom with him. It wasn't like he gave me a choice. So I curled up in a ball and pretended like I was asleep, and as soon as he fell asleep, I was outta there. I'm not going back until Mom's out . . . I mean *back.*" Dinah gave me a penetrating glare. I decided not to ask. Then she swung around the branch and stuck the landing of a perfect dismount. "Ta-Da!" she sang, throwing her hands up in the air and then taking a bow.

I jumped off the branch I was sitting on and landed in the grass on my hands and knees. I scuffled to my feet and dusted myself off. "Do you want to come stay at my house?" I offered, not sure if it would be better to suggest she could sleep on the couch or in my bed with Mark in the room. We didn't have any girls' rooms.

"No way!" Dinah nearly shouted at me as she grabbed both of my shoulders. "I told you. You can't tell anybody about me." She let go of me and reached for her backpack. "I mean it, Matthew. Any adult would report me to Welfare, and I'd end up in a foster home. You don't know how hard it would be for my mom to get me back." Her eyes pleaded as she looked up at me. "You promised. Anyway, it's only until July 9. I just need to lay low and stay cool for a couple of weeks."

She pulled an index card out of her back pocket and showed it to me. I recognized the sandwich bag it was wrapped in. On the card was a handwritten calendar counting down the days until July 9. Someone had scribbled "60 do 30" at the top. Dinah moved her thumb to cover the "60 do 30" and said, "See. Only 20 more days."

"So what can I do to help?" I asked earnestly.

"I don't need help," Dinah snapped. I must have looked hurt because she quickly added, "I'll tell you what I could use, though, is a can opener. Do you know where I can borrow a can opener?" She raised her eyebrows and grinned. "I'll give it back in 20 days."

"Actually, I do," I said. "There are at least three of them in the drawer in the church kitchen. Nobody would even notice if we borrowed one for a couple of weeks. Come on."

❦ Five ❦

I HEADED TOWARD the bike trail. For a second I thought about going back to the library to get my bike. But Dinah didn't have a bike, and I wasn't sure how long she'd follow me. I decided the faster I got to the can opener, the better.

"Where's your church?" Dinah asked, looking up and down the trail.

"It's Peace Congregation, just a little ways up this path," I told her, pointing up the hill, away from the library.

"Do you have a key?" asked Dinah.

"Nah," I said. "I won't need one. The front door will be unlocked. My dad will be there working on tomorrow's sermon."

Dinah froze in her tracks. "Whoa!" she cried, shaking her head.

"It's okay," I said. "He'll be up in his office. If he sees me, I'll just say that I stopped by to practice the piano."

"And where am I supposed to be?" Dinah just stood there with her eyes all popped out.

"We'll sneak around the back." I motioned for her to keep walking. "There's an old elm tree and dumpster near the back door. You can wait there, and then I'll come get you."

Dinah still didn't move. Instinctively, I took her hand and led her on. She didn't object. As soon as she was moving again, I let her hand drop. But the warmth of her hand stayed with mine.

The first thing we saw as we walked up to the church was the tall white steeple. There's a bell in the steeple that rings loud enough that you can hear it from Kyle's room a mile away. Usually I'm the one who rings the bell on Sunday mornings. There's a big, coarse rope like you use for tug-of-war, and you have to yank it real hard, then let it yank you back, then yank it again.

From inside the church with the doors shut, it doesn't sound so loud. But one time when Dad was marrying some people from out of town—no kids allowed—I went to stay with Kyle. They rang the bells after the ceremony, only they didn't even sound like the same bells to me. "What's that?" I asked Kyle. I was trying to figure out what other church around us had bells like that.

"Somebody's yanking your rope, dude!" laughed Kyle. I wondered what Kyle would say about Dinah. Part of me was almost glad he wasn't around to tell me what he thought. I wanted to sort this one out by myself.

The trail passed right by the church. I showed Dinah to the back door that led down a short stairway to the kitchen area of the basement. I turned the doorknob just to be sure. Locked as always. The only time anyone ever used it was to put the trash in the dumpster for pickup on Thursdays. Once last winter when I was helping Dad put out all the trash, I accidentally locked us out. We raced around to the front to get back in before we froze.

"Wait here," I told Dinah.

She nodded and leaned up against the dumpster. "Just hurry, okay?"

"Don't worry. I'll be right back."

I dashed around to the front of the church. It took me a moment to catch my breath, then I pulled open one of the glass doors and stepped inside, holding the bar down behind to keep it from clanking as it closed.

I could hear Dad's powerful preaching voice muffled through his closed office door: "So Jesus made a whip-puh out of cord-suh and drove all of the animal-suh from the Temple-uh saying, 'Get these out of here-uh! How dare you turn my Father's house-uh into a marke-tuh!' Yes, my brothers and sister-suh, our zeal for God's house-uh should consume us!" Sometimes when Dad practiced his sermons, he dragged out his words just like Grandpa. He never did that when he preached, though.

As I plodded down the steps to the basement, an idea began bouncing around in my brain. The thought gained momentum, and I did too. I ran through the kitchen, up the steps and burst through the back door, hanging on to the door as I swung around, so it wouldn't close behind me. Dinah was so startled that she dropped flat on the grass by the dumpster.

"Matthew!" she hissed. "Are you crazy? I nearly peed my pants!"

"Sorry," I apologized. Then we both cracked up. We laughed so hard I thought I was going to pee *my* pants.

"Did you get it?" she asked finally, looking puzzled by my empty hands.

"Even better," I said. "I have an idea. Come inside so we don't get locked out. It's okay. Nobody will see us."

"You first," Dinah said hanging on my shoulders as she followed me down the steps. "So what's your idea?"

"The church is completely empty every night. It's got bathrooms, and a kitchen, and look, over here is the youth rec room." The rec room wasn't much to look at really. Just a corner of the basement covered with carpet samples that had been duct-taped together, half a dozen beanbag chairs, a shelf of books and CDs, and a boom box.

"It's not exactly a Holiday Inn, but it's comfortable and dry. And it's got to be safer than sleeping in the park."

Dinah still looked skeptical, but she wandered across the carpet squares to check out the books and music.

"All we have to do is leave that back door unlocked," I went on. "You can lock it at night while
you're here. And I can make sure I'm here to take the
trash out on Wednesday nights. No one will even notice. What do you think?"

"Where did these come from?" Dinah was running
her fingers along the leaves of a plastic palm tree.

"They used to be up in the sanctuary. We moved
them down here for our winter beach party in February. As soon as we did, my mom put four live peace lily
plants there instead. I offered to put them back, but my
mom said, 'Over my dead body!'"

"They're perfectly hideous!" snickered Dinah.

"Yeah," I laughed. "Aren't they great?"

Dinah pulled two beanbags together and tested
them out like a bed. "Well, it is more comfortable than
the park," she conceded.

"There's even a couch up in the nursery where you
could sleep if you wanted to. There's a sofa in my dad's
office, too, but I think it would be better if you didn't
go up there." Dina was up looking through the CDs.
"So what do you think?"

"Have you ever spent the night here?" Dinah asked.

"Once—when we had a rock-a-thon to raise money for the new youth center. Twenty of us sat in rocking chairs rocking all night long. We made about $500." A vision of Kyle lying across a beanbag on top of his rocker while the rest of us rocked our hearts out and his sister's Electric Amish CD blared, *"Talkin' 'bout my congregation . . . my congregation"* made me smile.

"What time do I need to be out of here in the morning?" Dinah asked, pulling herself up out of the beanbags.

"Dad comes over and unlocks the doors at 8:00," I said. "Do you have a watch?"

"I have a watch, but no alarm." Dinah pulled a wristwatch out of her backpack.

"There's a timer in the kitchen." I said. "You can set that for however many hours you want to sleep."

"What if I get caught?" Dinah worried.

"You won't get caught. Just don't turn any lights on near the windows after dark. And if you hear someone, you can run out the back door and down the trail." Suddenly, I was afraid she might disappear forever. "Then we'll meet up again at the big maple tree behind the library, where we just had lunch."

As we walked back through the kitchen, I opened one of the drawers. "Here's where the can openers are," I said. "And here's the timer on top of the stove."

"I think I'll take a can opener with me," said Dinah. I nodded.

We bounded up the steps and I unlocked the door, making sure the button was all the way out. "It's all set," I told her.

"Thanks," said Dinah.

As we approached the trail, I pointed in the other direction. "See that light green house with the dark shutters? That's where I live. It's about two miles away by car, but hardly a minute's walk through the grass."

We walked back toward the library in perfect stride. This time we took the trail all the way around to the front of the library where my bike was parked.

"The library's closed tomorrow," Dinah reminded me.

"Then I'll meet you outside the back door of the church around 3:00. There's never anyone around on Sunday afternoons." I hesitated. "Do you want me to bring you something to eat?"

"That's okay . . . I've got cans of stuff to open, and I can pick up some bread outside the bakery at closing time. Thanks for lunch, though. And for a safe place to sleep tonight."

∽ Six ∾

THAT NIGHT, AS I was lying in bed, I searched my mind. Mark's steady breathing was pacing my flow of thoughts. *Inhale—exhale. Inhale—exhale. Di—nah. Di—nah.* There was a Dinah in the Bible. I pulled my flashlight out from under my bed and began leafing through the Old Testament. There she was. Genesis, Chapter 34. *Dinah and the Shechemites. Shechemites. Sounds like they're checking for bugs.* I began reading: "Now Dinah, the daughter Leah had borne to Jacob, went out to visit the women of the land. When Shechem son of Hamor the Hivite, the ruler of that area, saw her, he took her and violated her."

"Whoa!" Dinah's voice from this afternoon echoed through my brain. He *violated* her. I read the entire chapter about Dinah. Turns out Shechem actually loved Dinah, but her brothers were mad about the whole thing. They tricked Shechem into thinking he could marry Dinah as long as he and all of his men agreed to be circumcised. Shechem agreed, but after they all got circumcised and were in too much pain to fight, Dinah's brothers killed them all.

I remember when Johnny came home from the hospital. The first time I saw Mom changing his diaper I asked her what was wrong with his dobby. (That's what Mom calls it. Boys have dobbies, and girls have mollygobblers.) "The doctor circumcised Johnny," Mom told me.

"Why?" I asked, trying to figure out what the word meant.

"So it's easier to keep him clean," Mom explained.

"Am I circumcised?" I asked.

"All of my boys are circumcised," Mom said. But I don't remember it. I guess it's a good thing, because I bet if you remember it, it really hurt.

I turned back to Genesis. Funny—there's nothing else about Dinah. Nothing about how it felt to be violated. Or whether she decided she loved Shechem, too, after the whole violation thing. Or how she felt about her brothers killing him. Their father Jacob wasn't too happy about it. He thought all of the Canaanites would be mad and destroy his whole family.

My family says the Bible has all the answers. So why did it always leave me with more questions?

Last March when Dad was away on a mission trip, Grandpa gave the Sunday sermon. The title in the bulletin was, "The Truth, the Whole Truth, and Nothing but the Truth." I tried to pay attention because Grandpa always liked to discuss his sermons. Mostly he just talked about the Bible being the Word of God.

Afterward at dinner he asked Mom, "So what did you think of the sermon?"

"It's always good to get a different perspective," Mom replied.

"Perspective-uh!" Grandpa bellowed. "It's not about perspective-uh! Almighty God-duh said it and that settles it."

Mom looked at me, and then back to Grandpa. "What if there's more to God than what a handful of Jewish men could put into words?"

"Blasphemy!" exclaimed Grandpa. He pounded his fist on the table as he said it. That scared Johnny, and he started crying.

"If you'll excuse me," Mom said. She stood up and picked up Johnny. They walked away from the table with Mom bouncing Johnny on her hip until he quieted down.

"Would anyone like more mashed potatoes?" asked Grandma.

"No, thank you," Mark and I said in unison.

Grandpa turned to me. "Son, you know-wuh that the Bible is the absolute truth-uh, don't you?"

"Yes, sir," I managed to say. I could feel my ears burning.

"Everything you ever need to know is right there in the Good Book," said Grandpa.

"Yes, sir," I remember saying.

So I read the story of Dinah again, looking for clues. Then I flipped through the rest of the book of Genesis. There was definitely nothing else about Dinah. If all of the answers to my questions were there, I sure couldn't find them.

A gigantic yawn overpowered my thoughts. I slipped the flashlight and Bible back under my bed. My mind drifted from Dinah in the Bible to my Dinah, back to the Canaanites. From the land of Canaan. Land of Canines. And that night, I dreamed about Dinah and old Mrs. Miller's dogs.

ભ Seven ભ

SUNDAY SCHOOL AND church took forever. I kept looking around for signs that Dinah was there, had been there. The whole thing seemed like a dream. Mark's elbow in my ribs brought me back to the service. "Watch it!" I whispered loudly. Mark stuck his tongue out at me as he passed me the offering plate. I handed it to Mom, keeping it out of Johnny's reach.

During the sermon I looked at all of the people in the sanctuary. None of them had any idea that our church had its very own houseguest. I didn't think God would mind. He would want Dinah to be warm and safe and dry. And I liked the feeling that God was in on the secret.

Dinah was waiting for me at 3:00 behind the church. She had her backpack over her shoulder, but it didn't look nearly as full as it had the past two days. "Hey, Matthew!" she smiled.

"So what do you think?" I asked as we walked in the back door.

"It was weird at first," Dinah admitted, "but I fell asleep pretty early and didn't hear anything until the timer went off at 6:30." She pointed to the stove. "I think my favorite part was waking up to a bathroom and fresh water." Dinah led the way to the rec area and pulled out two beanbags for us to sit on. "So, welcome to my new home," she laughed. As I sat down beside her she asked, "Are you sure we won't have any other visitors this afternoon?"

"Definitely," I assured her. "I always come on Sunday afternoons to practice piano, and there's never anyone here until Dad comes back at 6:30 to get ready for the 7:00 service."

"Can I listen to you practice?" Dinah asked.

"Are you sure you want to?" I didn't mind playing in front of the church, but the thought of playing for Dinah suddenly made me nervous. "I mean, I can practice later."

Dinah was already up and pulling me up with her. "I definitely want to hear you play. You lead the way."

My mind raced through my entire musical repertoire as I led Dinah up to the sanctuary. By the time we

reached the piano, I had decided to pull out my classical piano solos book. Beethoven's *Für Elise*—that would
be good. Seems like half of Johnny's toys play the song,
which sounds pretty good even as electronic beeps. At
least she might recognize it.

Dinah settled into the front pew, as I began playing
Für Elise. She remained completely silent through the
whole piece. Then when I was done she gave me a
standing ovation. "That was great!" she exclaimed.
"Keep practicing."

I turned to *Londonderry Air*, another traditional piece
that I thought she might recognize. I'd only played the
first four measures when she jumped up and cried,
"That's *Danny Boy*! What key are you playing in?"

I looked at the music—no sharps or flats. "C," I
said.

"Can I play with you?" asked Dinah, as she pulled a
harmonica out of her pocket.

"Sure," I replied, trying to hide my surprise. I didn't
know anyone who played the harmonica. As I began
playing again, the harmonica sweetly echoed the melody line I was playing. Dinah added a little riff at the
end, and I stood up and applauded for her. "That was

really good," I complemented her sincerely. "Did you just play it from memory?"

"Kind of," Dinah said. "Are there any other songs in that book I might know?"

Dinah joined me on the piano bench, and we began looking through the index of the songbook together. "This is all classical stuff, isn't it?" she asked looking a little disappointed.

"It is, but you might recognize some of it. How about *Ode to Joy*?" I asked flipping through the pages.

"Ludwig von Beethoven, *Symphony Number 9*, 4th Movement," Dinah read from the songbook. "Never heard of it," she said shaking her head. "How's it go?"

As I started playing, Dinah started nodding. "Yeah, I have heard that before."

"We sing it at church," I said, and began singing, "Joyful, joyful we adore thee, God of Glory, Lord of Love." I had to quit playing because I can't sing and play the piano at the same time.

She put the harmonica to her lips and began playing with her eyes closed. I stopped singing and turned back to the piano. When I tried to play with her though, I sounded awful. "What key are you playing in?" she asked.

"Two sharps—key of D," I said.

"Can you play it in the key of C? I only have a C harp," she said holding out the harmonica and pointing to a little C on the front to the left of the holes.

"A C harp?" I asked. "I thought you were playing a harmonica."

"Harmonica—blues harp—same thing," said Dinah. "They come in all different keys. C's the most common. Mine's a C harp."

"So you can't play in D?" I asked. This time I was disappointed.

"No. I'm trying to learn to play cross-harp so I can play things in the key of G, too, but it's kinda harder than I thought it would be." Dinah ran her fingers across the black piano keys and then back across the white keys. "I thought you could play in any key you wanted on the piano." The back of her hand had little cuts and bruises all over it. I looked at her other hand holding the harmonica. There was a Band-Aid on her left pinkie.

"Well, I have to play in whatever key the song is written in. I know professional musicians can look at a song written in one key and play it in another, but I can't," I confessed. "I'm still working on being able to play what's written in front of me."

"So what do you have written in the key of C?" Dinah asked. I started flipping through the songbook trying to find something else in C. Something that I could play.

"I know lots of hymns in C," I offered doubtfully. I mean, Dinah didn't seem like the hymn-playing type.

"So play something," she said.

I pulled out the hymn book and turned to *The Love of God*, a hymn that I'd practiced a lot to play for a special during the offering last month. Dinah watched my fingers and dipped her shoulders gently in rhythm. "I can do that," she said and began playing the song with me. This time she started out playing some kind of an accompaniment, but it wasn't long before she was playing the melody right along with me.

"Wow!" I said, staring at her when we were through. "Did you know that song, too?"

"Nope," she said. "Never heard it before."

"You can sight read music that well the first time through?" I was even more shocked.

"Nope," she said. "I can't read music at all. I just play by ear."

"How do you do that?" I asked.

"Well, that song really only had 3 chords in it—C, F, and G. I started out playing the chords, then after I heard the melody, I started playing that, too."

"That's amazing!" My voice echoed through the sanctuary. I was so impressed. Just looking at her, you'd never know that Dinah was some kind of musical genius.

"It's the same chord progression they use in blues and country and the old rock songs, too. It's not that amazing, Matthew," Dinah grinned. I couldn't tell if she was pleased with herself for impressing me so, or amused that I didn't already know that.

I continued flipping through the hymn book selecting songs with no sharps or flats that I could play without butchering. Dinah would listen to the melody and be able to play along by the second time through. I got so distracted listening to her that I made more mistakes than she did.

I couldn't believe it when I looked up at the clock behind us. It was after 5:00. "Hey, I better go before my mom sends Mark to get me for dinner."

"Okay," said Dinah. "See you at the library tomorrow?"

"Definitely. I gotta get started on my summer study project."

❧ Eight ❧

I WAS ALREADY buried in science books when Dinah arrived at the library that Monday morning.

"What are you studying?" Dinah asked as she sat down at the table across from me.

"Time dilation and the speed of light," I said, propping my head up in my hands.

"What for?" asked Dinah, examining the book closest to her.

"I have this theory that I'm hoping to prove, but it's turning out to be way more complicated than I thought." I flipped the book in front of me shut and sighed. "Did you know that a light year is a measure of distance, not time?"

Dinah shrugged. "So what's your theory?"

"I started reading Einstein's Theory of Relativity and how the only constant speed we know of is the speed of light." Dinah raised her eyebrows and opened her eyes wide, trying to take it all in. "It's like this," I explained. "Suppose I throw a ball to you at 50 miles per hour. The ball's traveling at 50 miles per hour, right?"

"Okay," agreed Dinah.

"Now suppose we're riding on a train that's traveling 50 miles per hour. I'm holding the ball, so you and me and the ball are all traveling at 50 miles per hour on the train, right?" I checked to make sure she was still with me.

"Right," Dinah said.

"Okay, now suppose I throw the ball to you at 50 miles per hour. You and I are still traveling at 50 miles per hour, but the ball is traveling at 100 miles per hour, right?" I was nodding, but Dinah wasn't convinced.

"Which way are you facing?" Dinah asked.

"What do you mean which way am I facing?" I thought she was just messing with me.

"I mean are you throwing the ball in the same direction the train's moving or do you have your back to the front of the train, throwing it back to me?" Dinah asked. She was serious, and suddenly it dawned on me what she meant.

"Let's say I'm facing the front of the train and throwing the ball in the same direction that the train's moving," I said.

"Okay, then I can see that the ball would be traveling 100 miles per hour," Dinah conceded.

"So how fast something is traveling is relative to how fast the things around it are traveling. And that's true for everything except light. Light always travels at 300,000 kilometers per second. If the train was traveling at 100,000 kilometers per second and had a light on the front of it, the light would still only travel at 300,000 kilometers per second. If you were on another train traveling toward the light at 100,000 kilometers per second and the train with the light wasn't moving, the light would still travel toward you at 300,000 kilometers per second."

"Well, that seems a little weird," Dinah said. "So what's time dilation?"

"Time dilation is how time slows down the faster you move. So if you were in a rocket zooming by earth, you wouldn't age as fast as I would here on earth," I explained.

"And that's what you're trying to prove?" Dinah asked, looking at me like my hair suddenly poofed up like Einstein's.

"No, Einstein already proved all that. I'm trying to prove that the Bible told us this way before Einstein figured it out," I said. My palms were getting sweaty. I suddenly wondered if quoting Bible verses to Dinah was such a great idea.

"You mean like Einstein's Theory of Relativity is written in the Bible?" Dinah asked.

"Not all spelled out exactly, but when I was reading all the stuff Einstein proved, I kept thinking of two things I'd read in the Bible—that God is light, and that 1,000 years on earth is like a single day to God. So I want to do the math to see if the time dilation traveling at the speed of light would be like one day equals 1,000 years."

"So is that like algebra, or geometry, or what?" Dinah wanted to know.

"That's what I'm trying to figure out. I thought that I just needed to look up how long a light year is and then compare the number of seconds in a thousand light years to the number of seconds in a single day on earth. Only a light year is how far light travels in a year. Distance, not time. Now I'm stuck."

"You just need to take a break," Dinah suggested. "Did you bring your lunch again?"

I suddenly realized that I was starving. "It's in my backpack," I told her.

"So what are you waiting for?" asked Dinah, swinging her backpack over her shoulder.

"You go ahead. I need to stack up these books and let Mrs. Cleary know that I'll be back after lunch to use them again. I'll meet you by the maple tree."

Dinah was already out the door by the time I finished stacking up my books. Mrs. Cleary was sitting behind the reference desk reading an *Oprah* magazine. "Mrs. Cleary?" I said, not waiting for her to look up. "Those are my books on the table over there, and I'll be back to use them again after lunch."

"That's fine, Matthew." She peered up at me over the dark black rim of her reading glasses. "We'll just let them be until you return."

☙ Nine ☙

DINAH HAD SETTLED in under the tree and was digging stuff out of her backpack when I arrived. "What have you got?" I asked.

She held out a dented canister of Pringles and a glass jar of green olives with no label. "Chips and olives. How about you?"

I sat down beside her. "I don't know. Let me see what Mom packed today." I pulled out my sack lunch and discovered another turkey and Swiss sandwich, a huge golden delicious apple, and some baby carrots in a baggie. "Want half a turkey and Swiss sandwich?" I offered.

"Sure," Dinah said. I bit into the apple, keeping my eyes on the sandwich in her hand while she chewed and swallowed her first bite.

"Does it have mayonnaise?" I asked, still chomping on my apple.

"Mustard," she replied. "And it tastes great!"

"I'll trade you the whole thing for some of your chips," I bargained.

"Are you sure?" Dinah asked. "You can have as many of my chips and olives as you want anyway."

"I don't know why Mom has to put mustard on sandwiches in the summer when she knows I like mayonnaise." I was looking for a little sympathy, but Dinah just tilted her head at me and smiled.

"Why don't you pack your own lunch if you don't like your mom's sandwiches?" Dinah asked.

Yeah, why don't I? Truth was, it had never occurred to me to pack my own lunch. Mom always packed sack lunches for us, and we just grabbed them out of the fridge on our way out the door. "Maybe you're right," I said. "And if I pack my own lunch, I can bring enough stuff for both of us." It was such a good idea; I couldn't believe I hadn't thought of it before.

Dinah just smiled as she polished off the sandwich. She was eating normally this time, not like when she pulled my sandwich out of the trash. "Want some olives?" she asked, handing me the jar.

"I only like the red stuffing," I said as I inspected the jar, wondering if she got it from a trash can, too. It looked like it had never been opened.

"That's okay," Dinah said. "You eat the pimento, and I'll eat the olive." She didn't have to offer twice. Mom always let me have any extra pimentos floating in the jar, but she'd have a cow if she caught me picking the pimentos out of the olives. I popped open the jar and fished out an olive. I couldn't decide the best way to get the pimento out, though. "Just suck it out. I don't care," laughed Dinah. I sucked out the pimento and handed the empty olive to her. She popped it right in her mouth. We got a rhythm going and emptied the jar in no time.

As we finished the rest of our lunch, I finally worked up the nerve to ask her about the food. "So where'd you get the chips and olives?"

"They were okay, weren't they?" she asked looking down at the empty olive jar.

"They were great. I was just wondering, I mean . . ." I almost wished I hadn't asked, but I really did want to know. I figured she either had to buy them, or steal them, or pull them out of a trash can, but who throws away unopened jars and cans of perfectly good food?

Nobody I know. I wasn't sure what I wanted the answer to be.

"Do you really want to know?" Dinah asked.

I started stuffing the trash into my lunch sack. "Yeah," I admitted. "I really do."

Dinah took a deep breath. "I've been checking out the dumpsters behind the grocery store after dark. You wouldn't believe the stuff they throw out. Perfectly good food. Just because the container it's in doesn't look perfect anymore. Or because it expired today, like the minute the clock strikes midnight it'll turn bad."

I studied Dinah's hands as she talked. So that's how they got so beat up. Digging through dumpsters.

"I stay away from meat and dairy stuff that can go bad just because it's been sitting too long in a hot dumpster, but all of the stuff in cans and jars is good food going to waste."

"The chips and olives were good," I had to admit. "So I guess that explains the can opener."

"Yep," Dinah nodded. She stretched her body out in the grass and propped her head up on her elbow. I settled in myself, using my backpack as a pillow.

"So what's the best thing you've found in a can?" I asked.

"Definitely the meat. Like chicken and tuna," Dinah said. "When I walked out of the church with that can opener, I sat right down and ate three cans of tuna."

"Good protein," I told her. Mom was always carrying on about growing boys needing lots of protein. I figured growing girls did, too.

"So what's the worst thing you've tried?" I felt like some kind of quiz show host asking question after question, working my way up to the million-dollar question.

"Mystery meat," Dinah said trying to sound serious. "I had one can without a label and when I opened it, I couldn't tell if it was some kind of hash or dog food. It smelled a lot like the Alpo the lady down the street used to feed her dog."

"Tell me you didn't eat the dog food!" I barked, and then howled like a wolf.

"I didn't eat the dog food," Dinah mimicked. "I dumped it out in the woods for the squirrels and coons." I wasn't sure how a raccoon sounded, so I did my best squirrel act. "So what are you now, a dog with rabies?" Dinah scrambled up the tree to escape.

So much for my squirrel. "I'm a hunting dog!" I cried. "And I just treed my first coon!" I'd never been hunting, but I read a book once about how they use dogs to chase raccoons up a tree after dark. The coon's eyes would shine orange in the night, and then they'd shoot them right between the eyes. I always thought it would be cool to have a coon skin hat, but I was pretty sure my parents wouldn't think so.

Next thing I knew, Dinah jumped out of the tree and tackled me. I tried to wrestle her down, but she had me pinned. "Okay, okay," I hollered. "You win!" Dinah laughed and let me go. As she walked back to her backpack, I asked, "Got your blues harp with you?"

"I do," Dinah nodded.

"Will you play something for me?" Yesterday, every song we played was something I knew. I wondered what kind of music she liked.

"Sure," Dinah said, digging around in her backpack for the harmonica. She pulled out the sleek black case with orange "C" stickers on at least three sides. She lifted the top of the case open and gently turned it over, laying the silver harmonica on the palm of her hand. It looked even shinier today than it did in the church yesterday. The harmonica fit perfectly in the crook of her left hand with two fingers on top and her thumb beneath. She cupped her right hand around the other end and began playing the sweetest melody I'd ever heard—sad but hopeful notes pouring out of the harmonica all together.

"So what's it called?" I asked when she finished playing.

"*Blowin' in the Wind*," she replied as she tapped the harmonica on her shorts, wiped it clean with her t-shirt, and carefully placed it back in the case. "Ready to hit the books?"

❧ Ten ❧

As I SLOWLY burrowed back into my stack of books, Dinah settled in on the opposite end of the table with a large book entitled *Blues Harp*. I started thinking of ways I might be able to put a time value on the speed of light. Time/Distance. Apples/Oranges. My mind was mush. I spent the next hour scanning the index of each book trying to think of a new angle.

Suddenly, a wad of paper hit my head and dropped on the table in front of me. I unwadded the paper to find a scribbled poem.

Food for Thot
As I sit in the library
Pondering intensely on the subject of Life
I realize
If Edgar Allen Poe
Had been named Allen Edgar Poe
We could call him "ALPO"
For short

I laughed. Feeling inspired, I drew a can with the word "ALPO" on it, a circle around it, and a line through it. I wadded it back up and flung it at Dinah, who was hiding behind the *Blues Harp* book. Bull's-eye!

As she was smoothing out my return message, I was thinking about her light toss versus my direct shot. An idea started to form about how to turn the measure of light years into a time measurement. *Light travels at 300,000 kilometers per second. Maybe I could calculate out how fast the earth is traveling through space, and then calculate how long it would take to travel 300,000 kilometers at that speed. Then convert the seconds into days and years to see if the ratio is the same as one day to 1,000 years. Brilliant!* I scribbled this brainstorm down in my notebook, so that I'd have it clear in my mind to start fresh tomorrow. As I was writing, Dinah came around behind me and said softly, "Meet you back by the tree."

"Okay," I whispered. "Just let me figure out what to do with all these books."

I stacked the books up—an even dozen. I had our family library card, but there was no way I wanted to haul them all home on my bike. But I didn't want them reshelved, either. I'd have to write down all the titles to be able to find them tomorrow and hope nobody else checked them out. I went over to talk to Mrs. Cleary.

Mrs. Cleary was checking out a bunch of DVD's for a lady and her kids. As soon as they were through, I explained my predicament. "Well, Matthew, how about if I give you one of these gray crates, and you put all of the books in there for tonight, and I'll keep them back here behind the desk for you until tomorrow?"

"That'd be great, Mrs. Cleary," I said. "Thank you."

"I'll just put this yellow sticky on top with your name, and nobody will bother it." Mrs. Cleary peered up over the top of her glasses at me. "So who's your new friend? I don't think I've seen her around here before this week. Someone new at Peace Congregation?"

My mind raced. Mrs. Cleary didn't attend Peace Congregation, but she knew my dad was the pastor, and she might say something to my mom the next time Mom was at the library. Plus there was my promise to Dinah not to say anything. Dinah kind of was someone new at Peace Congregation. She didn't attend any of the services, but she was living there, for crying out loud. I decided the less I said the better. I kind of shrugged my shoulders, nodded, and mumbled, "Yeah." Then I tried to change the subject. "I'll be in as early as I can tomorrow. Thanks again, Mrs. Cleary." And I was out the door.

I raced around the back of the library to find Dinah perched up in our maple tree. I dumped my backpack at the foot of the tree beside hers and scrambled up beside her. "You're not going to like this," I said as I wedged myself safely up against the tree trunk.

"What am I not going to like?" Dinah asked. She reached up to the branch above us and was looking down at me curiously.

"The librarian, Mrs. Cleary, just asked me about you," I told her. My heart was pounding.

"What did you say?" Dinah asked, and swung right down beside me again, almost knocking me off the limb.

"I didn't tell her anything," I said. "She asked me like three questions at once, and the last one was something like were you new at the church, and I was like 'yeah' and got out of there. I didn't tell her that you were staying at the church. I think she kind of assumed that your family just moved here and started going to my church." I was out of breath by the time I got it all out.

"That's definitely not good," Dinah frowned.

"I know," I agreed, taking a deep breath. "I'm afraid if she sees us together again, she'll mention it to my mom next time she sees her."

"So I guess I'm done at the library." Sadness weighed down Dinah's face. "That reeks!" she shouted at no one in particular. She grabbed a branch above her and shook the limb as hard as she could. The branch we shared bounced up as she pulled down and back down as she pushed up. Leaves and propellers abandoned the tumultuous branches in favor of solid ground. I hung on tight so as not to join them.

"I'm really sorry," I said. "What do you think we should do?"

Dinah jumped out of the tree, crushing a bunch of the leaves and seeds she just knocked down. "I think I shouldn't be hanging out at the library anymore," she said. "At least not with you. And not while Mrs. Cleary is around. Any idea when she's not working?"

I thought about it. "Well, she's here every morning when the library opens at 10:00." I climbed down out of the tree, hanging onto the limb and getting my feet close to the ground before dropping. "I doubt that she stays until it closes at 9:00. I don't really know what time she leaves, but I can show you where she parks her old blue Buick."

"That'll work!" Dinah's eyes brightened. "I can watch and see when she leaves. Lead the way!"

ᘓ Eleven ᘓ

DINNER THAT NIGHT revolved around Mark's pleas for a pair of Air Jordan Jumpman Jeter baseball training shoes.

"I don't know why I even let him try them on," Mom was saying to Dad.

"You said it yourself, Mom," Mark jumped in. "My feet are growing, and I'm going to need a good pair of men's shoes."

"I was talking about Sunday dress shoes, Mark," Mom said. "Your feet are still growing, and I can't see spending $100 on a pair of shoes you'll outgrow by the end of the year."

"I've never spent $100 on a pair of tennis shoes," Dad said.

"But they're not tennis shoes, Dad," Mark argued. "Nobody in our family even plays tennis. These are training shoes that I can wear anywhere." Mark was looking at me and shaking his head, trying to get me to help him out. "Everywhere except for church on Sunday," he added.

I rolled my eyes at Mark, looked down at my meatloaf and then turned to Mom. "May I have the ketchup, please?"

"We can't afford to spend $100 on a pair of shoes." Dad's face reddened as his voice got louder. "Look around the table. If we all bought a pair of shoes for $100, that would be $600. For $600 every closet in this house should be packed full of shoes!"

"How about $25 for a pair of shoes?" Mark countered.

Dad looked a little surprised, and I could see him letting down his guard. It wasn't like Mark to give up so easy. "Well, now, $25 is more like it, don't you think, Theresa?"

Mom wasn't buying it. "Which shoes did you like for $25?"

"Well, if you think about it, my outgrowing a shoe isn't really a problem," Mark began. He was trying to sound so reasonable; I could tell he hadn't given up on the Jordan-Jeter shoes yet. He was just regrouping and still hoping to win the war. "When I outgrow the shoes,

Luke will be able to wear them. Matthew may even be able to wear them for a while after I outgrow them."

That was a low blow! I glared at Mark. No way was I helping him now. Dad had leaned back in his chair. I could tell he was just going to let Mark chatter on until he ran out of steam. Mom looked at me and winked. Mark forged right on, though. "A quality pair of shoes like these Jumpman Jeters, well, Johnny will be able to wear them, and the new baby on the way, too. That's shoes for at least four, maybe five of us. So that's only $20 or $25 apiece."

Dad shook his head. "We're not buying a $100 pair of shoes for you, Mark. That's final."

"What if I earn the money myself?" Mark just couldn't take no for an answer.

"How are you going to do that?" Dad asked.

"Well, you could pay me to . . ."

Dad interrupted. "Mark, I already told you that it's not going to be my $100 that buys those shoes. Anything that you do for me, you do because you're a part of this family, and we all work together. I don't pay your mom or Matthew for everything they do, and I'm not going to start paying you. We take the money we have, and we use it to buy what we need. You need a new pair of shoes? We'll get you a new pair of shoes. But nobody needs a $100 pair of shoes. I understand you want them. You need to understand we're not buying them."

And that was that. I'm not sure Mark had figured it out yet, but he wasn't getting the Jordan Jumpman Jeter shoes.

I waited until after dinner when I was helping Mom clear the table to talk about packing my own lunches from now on. Finally the two of us were alone in the kitchen. "Mom," I asked, "what time in the morning do you get up and pack our lunches?"

"Oh, I'm usually up at 5:30, and I have the lunches packed by 6:30. Why?" Mom scraped the plates and handed them to me to put in the dishwasher.

"Would it be okay if I started packing my own lunch?" I knew she'd want to know why, and I'd been thinking about that. Sure enough, that was the first thing she asked.

"Why do you want to start packing your own lunch?" Mom really was kind of suspicious about everything.

"I just thought you might appreciate having one less thing to do . . . with the baby coming and all." I wasn't ready for too many questions. "And I know that I need to pack something healthy from each food group. It's not like you keep a lot of junk food around the house, anyway."

Mom brushed her hair out of her eyes with the back of her hand. The bigger the baby got, the more tired Mom always looked by the end of the day. I could tell she was ready to sit down and put her feet up during our after-dinner reading hour. "I don't see why not," she said, mussing my hair like she does with Johnny when she wants to make him laugh. "Guess my first baby's growing up." Mom smiled, and I was thinking that this might be a good time to go double or nothing.

"I was thinking, too, Mom, that I'm old enough and responsible enough now to have my own library card. I know that you'd have to sign for it and all, but I'd take really good care of it and of the books I check out."

Mom leaned back against the counter and took a deep breath. "Anything else?" she asked.

"Nope," I said. I knew I'd won and flashed her my best grin. "I'll bring home the form for you to sign tomorrow." She put her arm around my shoulder and pulled me toward her. Her belly was getting bigger every day, but I always felt like an only child again when Mom hugged me.

❧ Twelve ❧

I HAD MY own temporary library card by Wednesday morning, but I could only check out two books at a time until my permanent library card came in the mail. That was fine with me. I was packing my own lunch and sharing it with Dinah underneath our tree every day now. She always had interesting stuff to share. Beef jerky, squashed Twinkies—junk food my mother would never feed us, but that I felt obliged to eat so I wouldn't hurt Dinah's feelings. And the canned fruit was always good.

I couldn't wait to show Dinah my library card. She didn't know it yet, but I got it for her. We were munching on a box of Ritz crackers that had expired last week, when I flashed her my card.

"That's great, Matthew," she said, tilting her head at me and scrunching up her eyebrows. "I guess I thought you already had a library card."

"We have a family card," I said. "And my mom keeps a list of everything we check out for school and to make sure nothing's overdue. Now I can check out things on my own, and my mom won't necessarily know about it or ask me any questions."

Dinah's eyes lit up. She chugged some water to clear the crackers from her mouth. "So what are you going to check out first?"

"I can only check out two books at first, so I was thinking I could pick one, and you could pick one." I tried to sound casual about it, but I could tell she was excited.

"That would be great!" Dinah exclaimed. "I can finally practice the stuff I'm reading from that *Blues Harp* book while I'm reading it instead of trying to remember it all for later!" She reached inside her backpack for her notebook and tore out a sheet of paper.

"You'll need to write down the title and author so I can find it," I told her.

"I'll need to write down more than that," she chuckled. "I've been hiding the book in a section of old magazines nobody ever reads to make sure no one else finds it and checks it out."

I was pleased with myself for realizing that she didn't have a library card and wasn't going to draw attention to herself by applying for one. Not that her mother was around to sign for it. I'd been thinking about Dinah's mother a lot. I had tons of questions.

"Dinah, can I ask you a question?" I ventured.

"You just did," she replied. Her eyes told me that I could ask her another one, but not too much.

"I was just wondering if your mother wouldn't be worried—you know, if she called Jerry's apartment and found out you're not there," I stammered.

"I've been thinking about that, too," Dinah confessed. "I wrote her a letter, and I've spent hours digging through the trash outside the post office thinking I might find some stamps, but no luck. I was thinking tonight I'd walk down to the mall and try to collect enough money out of the fountain to buy a stamp. I just have to be extra careful about mall security."

"I have a whole book of stamps at home," I told her. "Mom got them for me before my friend Kyle left for the summer so I could write to him whenever I want. Do you want me to mail it for you?" I really wanted to see the address on the envelope so I'd know where her mom was.

"How about if you just bring me a stamp tomorrow?" Dinah suggested.

I nodded and tried not to look disappointed. "I can do that."

"Do you want to read it?" Dinah asked, taking me completely by surprise.

"Yeah, sure. If that's okay."

She handed me the letter, but there was no envelope and no address.

Dear Mom,

I miss you, and I hope that you're doing okay. I'm counting the days until July 9. Please don't worry about me. I'm having a good summer. I spend lots of time at the library with my new friend Matthew. He's a couple of years younger than I am, but very smart and very sweet. He's trying to teach me about the speed of light and Einstein's Theory of Relativity.

Do they let you go outside at all? I bet you miss walking barefoot in the grass at the park. I've been doing that every day for you. It makes me feel like you're right here with me. I know you will be soon.

I'll see you at Jerry's at noon on July 9.

Love,

Dinah

XXOOXXOO

P.S. I wrote you this poem:
He is so young
And yet so tall
With perfect shape and form

The sun's his love
The clouds his hope
And he enjoys a storm

There's millions more
That seem like him
Tho different in a way

A blade of grass
That's what he is
The beauty of one day

I read the letter silently and didn't know what to say when I was through. It sounded like her mom was locked up in a mental institution somewhere. No wonder Dinah didn't want to talk about it. Creepy Jerry probably drove her crazy. I wondered what they could do to her to make her sane again by July 9. Surgery maybe, or electric shocks? Now I really wanted to see that address on the envelope.

76

"Nice poem," I said. "I liked your Alpo poem, too. How many poems have you written?"

"I wrote one for you last night," Dinah replied. She flipped back through her notebook, tore out another page, and handed it to me.

Poor Old Soul
In a dark and dusty corner
Alone and very cold
He sits there feeling useless
All worn out and old

His tongue has never spoken
His eyes have never seen
His sole is worn and weary
He's lost all self-esteem

No one wants him since he's old
What's left for him to do?
His usefulness left long ago
That poor old tennis shoe

"You wrote that for me?" I liked it, but I didn't get it.

"For you and your brother and his $100 shoes," Dinah said.

I laughed. I forgot I told her about that. Even after Dad had told him definitely not, Mark lay in bed and went on and on about the full-grain leather and the air-soles and the fancy eye-stay system and the plush tongue with its lockdown performance fit. "But it's not just a tennis shoe," I said, mocking Mark. "It's an Air Jordan Derek Jeter Jumpman—the ultimate baseball training shoe!"

"All for only $50 each!" chimed in Dinah. We danced around, kicking our feet up and laughing as we cleaned up our lunch trash.

"I'll throw that in the garbage on my way back in the library," I said. "Want to meet back here in an hour? I'll have your harmonica book for you."

"That's so sweet of you, Matthew," Dinah said. Happiness surged through my body.

"Do you want another book to read, too? I don't really need to take any of those science books home. Mrs. Cleary's letting me keep them behind the desk." I was looking down and kind of kicking the ground with my sneaker as I said it. "Anyway, it won't be long before

I'll have the real card. Then I can check out as many books as I want."

"Are you sure you don't mind?" Dinah asked.

"I don't mind at all," I answered, smiling. I found myself smiling a lot when I was with Dinah. "What book do you want to read?"

I was back an hour later with the harmonica book and the first Harry Potter book, *Harry Potter and the Sorcerer's Stone*. Peace Congregation did not care for magic, wizardry, or Harry Potter. But there wasn't anyone from Peace there when I checked it out, and it wasn't like I was planning on lugging it all around with me or reading it myself. I just borrowed it for a friend.

"Don't forget, tonight's trash night," I told Dinah before I left. "Church will be done by 9:00, and I'll stay after and help with trash and make sure the back door stays unlocked, okay?"

"Thanks, Matthew," Dinah said, as she packed the books away.

"And I'll bring that stamp for you tomorrow," I added. "Stay out of the fountain and away from mall security."

❧ Thirteen ❧

MOM CAME INTO the kitchen just as I finished packing my lunch.

"Let's see what you've got," Mom said.

I swallowed hard and handed her the bag. She peered inside at my two turkey and Swiss sandwiches (one with mustard and one with mayonnaise), an apple, a banana, at least a dozen baby carrots, and two string cheese sticks. I held my breath.

"My goodness, Matthew," Mom said. "I suspected there was something you weren't telling me when you wanted to pack your own lunch. I had no idea that I wasn't giving you enough food!" She rolled the paper bag shut and handed it back to me. "You must be coming up on another growing spurt."

"Thanks, Mom," I said, heading for the door.

"Oh, Matthew," Mom called after me. "There's a letter from Kyle in this morning's mail. It's on the stand in the entryway."

"Got it!" I yelled back. I grabbed the letter and stuffed it in my backpack. I rode as fast as I could to the library. I went straight back to our tree and found Dinah lying in the grass on her stomach studying the harmonica book.

"So I guess the blues harp is more interesting than Harry Potter," I said as we nodded hello.

"Nah," she said, as she sat up and handed me the Harry Potter book. "I finished this over an hour ago. I was hoping you could get me Year Two today."

"You read this whole book in a day?" I couldn't believe it. I turned to the back of the book. "It has over 300 pages!"

"Not like I have anything else to do," Dinah laughed.

I flipped through the Harry Potter book. Maybe once I got my real library card, I'd check it out again and read it myself. It must be pretty good or Dinah wouldn't read it so fast and be ready for the next one.

I put Harry Potter in my backpack and pulled out Kyle's letter and Dinah's stamp. "Here's your stamp," I said as I handed it to her. "I got a letter from Kyle."

"So how's Kyle liking life on the farm?" Dinah asked.

"I don't know. I grabbed it on the way out and haven't had a chance to read it yet." I tore the letter open. "Want to hear it?" I thought it was only fair that I share my letter with her, since she let me read her letter to her mom yesterday. Plus Kyle can be pretty entertaining.

"Sure," Dinah said. She lay on her back, her arms behind her head and the harmonica book open across her chest. I cleared my throat and began reading.

Dear Matthew,

Hey! How's it going? Me, not too bad. Grandpa says he'll make a farmer of me by the end of summer. I don't think so.

Grandpa milks the cows at 4:30 every day. That's 4:30 AM and 4:30 PM. He hauled me out of bed to milk with him the first morning, but then Grandma convinced him I'm a growing boy and need my sleep. Thank you, Grandma!

The worst part is the smell. Sometimes it stinks so bad I have to pull my shirt over my nose and mouth to keep from hurling.

Grandpa laughs and says that's the smell of money and I'll learn to love it. I definitely don't think so.

They got me all confused over mealtimes here. Grandma kept asking me what I want for dinner and then making it for lunch. Took me three days to figure out they eat breakfast, dinner, and supper, not breakfast, lunch, and dinner like us.

They call cantaloupes muskmelons and green peppers mangos. The milk's not pasteurized, and we skim the cream right off the top. I churned some of it into butter. Grandma acted like it was the best butter she ever tasted, but it wasn't as good as a stick of store butter.

Anyway, Grandma wants to fatten me up and Grandpa wants to work me 'til I'm skin and bones, so you'll know who won when you see me in August.

Am I missing anything fun? Any news if Acts is a boy or girl yet? Well, I gotta go chop wood. It's 85 degrees outside and Grandpa's worrying about freezing in February. WRITE ME BACK!!!

Your friend,

Kyle

When I finished reading the letter, Dinah asked me, "So who's Ax?"

"Acts is what Kyle calls the new baby," I told her.

"Ax like you use for cutting wood? What kind of name is Ax for a baby?" Dinah scrunched up her eyebrows and frowned.

"It's just Kyle's weird sense of humor," I laughed. "And it's Acts, like Acts of the Apostles, not ax like a hatchet." I stood up and headed down toward the creek.

"I still don't get it," Dinah said, following me.

"My parents named me Matthew. My brothers are Mark, Luke, and John. Like the gospels," I explained. "The first four books of the New Testament. It's Matthew, Mark, Luke, John, then the next book is Acts." I kicked a walnut toward my reflection in the creek and watched my face disappear in the splash.

"Would your parents really name a baby Acts?" Dinah asked.

"Nah," I told her, although suddenly I wondered myself. "No," I repeated with more conviction. "Nobody but Kyle would call a baby Acts." I kicked another walnut, only this time I missed my reflection. I watched as the circles rippled through my head and down my body.

"So you're named after a book of the Bible?" Dinah parked herself and her backpack by the edge of the creek and began taking off her shoes and socks.

"Yes—well, after the Apostle Matthew, I guess. What about you?" I'd been wondering about that ever since I read about Dinah in Genesis. That was one name from the Bible Mom and Dad definitely wouldn't pick for a girl. I couldn't imagine why Dinah's mom had picked that name.

"My name's Dinah Renae. My mom's name is Rose Dinah. Her mom picked the name Dinah because she loved Dinah Shore." Dinah leaned back on her elbows and splashed her feet in the creek. "Mom said in her family, the mom's middle name is automatically her daughter's name. Her mom's name was Frances Rose. And her grandma's name was Mary Frances. So Mary Frances had Frances Rose, and Frances Rose had Rose Dinah, and she had Dinah Renae." Dinah alternated the splashing her feet with each generation. "My daughter will be Renae, and then I'll get to pick my granddaughter's name when I pick my daughter's middle name. Get it?"

"Who's Dinah Shore?" I asked.

"Dinah Shore—you know, the singer, golf tournament lady, TV star?" Dinah told me.

I shook my head. "Sorry. I've never heard of her."

"Well, she's been dead a while, so I guess maybe you wouldn't have," Dinah conceded. "She was a great singer and TV star. I've been reading up on her here at the library and listening to some of her songs in the audio room.

"So that's who you were named after—a dead singer and golfer?" It didn't sound like something I'd be too proud of.

"Well, she wasn't dead when my grandmother picked that name. Dinah Shore's real name was Frances Rose Shore. Frances Rose, just like my grandmother." Dinah looked at me closely to make sure I was interested or at least following. I stopped kicking nuts into the creek and sat down beside her. "When Dinah Shore was still Frances Rose Shore she sang that song that goes 'Dinah won't you blow, Dinah won't you blow, Dinah won't you blow your horn.'"

Dinah sang the entire chorus for me. Her voice was somewhere between a tenor and an alto. Not that I expected her to be a soprano.

"You know that song?" Dinah asked. I nodded. "Well, the announcer forgot her name when she sang that song on the radio and started calling her Dinah. She decided she liked that better than Frances Rose and just called herself Dinah after that."

"So you're named after a dead singer who was named after a train?" I was feeling better and better about the names my parents chose.

"I'm named after Dinah Shore," Dinah corrected me, "and Dinah Shore was actually a pioneer among women. You wouldn't believe all the stuff I've been reading about her."

I had the feeling she was going to tell me anyway, so I got comfortable before I asked, "Like what?"

"Well, to start off with, Dinah Shore had polio when she was young. She exercised so hard that she learned to walk without a limp. She was a really good tennis player and golfer." I had to admit that was impressive. She must have been pretty athletic to begin with, though. More like Mark than like me. Like Dinah, too. She was sure good at getting up and down trees. Muscular, like a gymnast, not scrawny like me. Dinah was still going on about Dinah Shore. I started looking for smooth rocks that we could skip.

She talked about Dinah Shore like she was a member of her own family. I had never heard anyone talk like that about somebody they never even met and who died before we were even born. But I guess when you don't have much of a family yourself, maybe you should get to adopt other people's family history. I just leaned back and let her keep chattering until she told me everything she thought I needed to know about Dinah Shore.

I was kind of listening to Dinah, and kind of writing my letter back to Kyle in my head. *Not much to write about if I leave out Dinah.* So I started thinking about how to convert light years from distance to time again. *Maybe I should calculate how many seconds there are in a year. Then I could calculate how far light would travel in a year and compare that to how far the earth travels around the sun in a year.*

Dinah interrupted my strategy. "So do you want to eat lunch early, or study in the library a while? It's only 10:30."

"I don't care," I said, sitting up and stretching. A big yawn followed. "How about you?"

"I'm okay for now," Dinah decided. "I'd like to be able to read Harry Potter Year Two while you're studying in the library."

"All right," I said. I'll meet you back by the tree in a little bit."

✂ Fourteen ✂

DINAH AND I settled into a comfortable routine over the next week. She played her harmonica with me when I practiced on Sunday, and she read the whole Harry Potter series that week. I wanted it to be June forever, but suddenly it was July first.

We finished dinner as usual, and Luke was jumping up on Dad shouting, "A horse! A horse! My kingdom for a horse!" That's what we always said to get Dad to be our horse.

But Dad said, "Sorry, Luke. I've got a meeting to go to." Dad never had meetings on Thursday nights. "Come give me a kiss and hug goodnight." Dad wasn't planning to be home before their bedtime.

"Where are you going?" I asked as he kissed Mom goodbye and kissed the baby in her belly goodbye. My heart stopped. *Please don't let it be the church.*

"I've got a meeting at the church," he said and gave me a goodnight hug, too. "I shouldn't be too late, but Johnny and Luke will definitely be in bed asleep." He picked up his briefcase and car keys.

"How come you're driving if the meeting's at the church?" I asked.

"They're calling for thunderstorms tonight. I'd better drive just in case." And with that he was gone.

At 9:00 Mom sent Mark and me to bed. There was still no sign of Dad. I peered out the window. Just looking at the back of the church, I couldn't tell whether the meeting was still going or not.

"What are you looking at?" Mark asked.

"The clouds," I said. "Dad said it's supposed to storm tonight." I closed the curtains and nestled into bed.

"I sure hope it doesn't flood the ball field." Mark propped himself up on his elbows. "We need to practice for the Fourth of July Tourney this weekend."

"Is baseball the only thing you care about?" I asked him.

"Heck, no!" Mark retorted. "I care about soccer and basketball, and I like swimming, too."

"Anything else?" I asked shaking my head.

"I've been thinking more about winter sports. Maybe hockey or even downhill skiing."

"Good night, Mark," I said and pretended to go to sleep so Mark would, too.

"Night," said Mark. I watched the clock. This had already been the longest night of my whole, entire life. I didn't know it yet, but it was really just starting.

Lightning illuminated the room. In the flash, I saw Mark sleeping. The thunder boomed not far behind, but Mark didn't stir. Just as the patter of raindrops started, I heard the garage door open. I crept silently down the stairs, just far enough to hear better, but not far enough for Mom and Dad to see me. I heard the garage door close, then voices in the kitchen. I couldn't make out what they were saying until they came into the living room and sat on the couch.

"Looks like you were right about that storm," Mom said.

"The storm outside doesn't begin to compare to the tempest at church tonight." Dad sounded weary.

"So, did you get anything resolved?" Mom asked.

"The deacons voted seven to five to let Mrs. Miller bring her dogs to church in exchange for funding the building project," Dad told her. "Nobody wants to open the sanctuary up to any and all dogs, but it is hard not to bow to the almighty dollar."

"Bow?" Mom laughed. "More like bow-wow!" Mom was still trying to be funny, but Dad wasn't laughing. "So, are we just charging admission for dogs?"

"I'm afraid it's worse than that." Dad sighed. "The official vote was that given Mrs. Miller's advanced age and fragile condition, she is disabled, and her dogs are service dogs. By law, we have to admit assistance dogs for the disabled—guide dogs for the blind, hearing dogs for the deaf, and service dogs for the physically disabled," Dad explained. "The dogs will wear a special harness or backpack to identify them as service dogs. Mrs. Miller has already obtained authorization for handicapped parking."

"That's not so bad, is it, Paul?" Mom asked.

"I haven't gotten to the bad part yet," Dad said. I could hear the wind picking up outside, and I was glad that there was lightning to forewarn me of the crashing thunder. I moved further down so I could see my parents, too.

"Mrs. Miller also announced that her health is deteriorating," Dad went on.

"Mrs. Miller was at the meeting?" Mom sounded truly surprised.

"Ben Arnold told her about the meeting, and she took it upon herself to attend," Dad explained. "She implied that she's getting her affairs in order and would leave at least another million to Peace Congregation if the church sees fit to comfort and support her in this difficult time."

"What kind of comfort and support is she looking for?" Mom asked.

"She's getting the guesthouse ready so she can hire a personal assistant to stay on the property with her. She's hired Tom Stone to install an intercom system next week, including the guesthouse and the house, and to make sure everything in the house is in working order." Dad paused. "And she wants me to interview the applicants, and would like to have someone lined up by the end of the month. I'm to run the ad in Sunday's classified section."

"You would have done that for her anyway, wouldn't you?" asked Mom. Dad stood up and started pacing.

"That's exactly my point!" Dad said with sweeping gestures he usually saved for behind the pulpit. I slid back up a few stairs to be safe. "Here is a longstanding member of our congregation who either thinks she has to hold money over our heads for us to treat her with simple Christian charity, or who thinks that she can buy her way into Heaven as well as everything she wants from the church along the way."

"God is not a respecter of persons," Mom quoted scripture.

"That's just the confirmation I was looking for," Dad said as he sat down and put his arm around Mom. "I think it's time for a little reminder that God loves us all just the same and isn't impressed by anybody's money. First thing tomorrow morning, I'm rewriting my Sunday Independence Day sermon."

I was just ready to head back to bed when I heard Dad say, "Oh, the back door of the church was unlocked when I went to take a bag of trash out to the dumpster. I'm sure Matthew told me he locked it last night. I have no idea who would have unlocked it today. Was there a women's meeting in the basement I didn't know about this afternoon?"

"Not that I know of," replied Mom.

"Hmmm," Dad pondered. "Well, it's locked now."

Dad locked the door! Dinah's locked out!

❧ Fifteen ❧

My mind raced. I had to find Dinah and get her back into the church where she'd be safe from the storm. I hurried back up to my room. Thank God Mark sleeps like a human vegetable. I put some clothes and my flashlight in a bag. Then I sat at the top of the steps and waited for Mom and Dad to go to sleep. I didn't move until my dad had been snoring for a full five minutes.

I slipped into the kitchen and opened the drawer where Dad kept the car keys. I knew there was both a front door and back door key to the church on that key ring. Once I had the keys in my hand, I stopped to make sure Dad was still snoring and that there was no sign of Mom. *All I have to do if I get caught is hide the clothes bag, open the refrigerator, and say I'm hungry. Mom will definitely buy that since I'm still in my pajamas and she thinks I'm having a growing spurt.*

I saw lightning flash just as I was ready to open the door to the garage, so I waited for the thunder to make my escape. It was pitch black in the garage. I thought about turning on the light in the garage, but it seemed too risky. I fished around inside my bag and pulled out the flashlight. I changed into my clothes as quickly as possible, stuffed my pajamas into the bag, and hid the bag in the cabinet where Mom kept all the extra toilet paper, Kleenex, and diapers.

I debated about whether or not to ride my bike, but decided since Dinah was walking, I'd better walk, too. I grabbed Mark's rain poncho out of his baseball bag and mine out of the cabinet. *Should I take Dad's big Notre Dame umbrella out of the car? I might as well walk around with a key on a kite waiting for lightning to strike me.* I slipped into my rain poncho and stuffed Mark's poncho inside the big front pocket. Then I stepped quietly out into the night.

The rain was really coming down. I darted through the torrents, straight across the grass to the church. I ran faster, driving even more rain into my face. The drops rolled, dripped, and splashed into my eyes. The uneven ground knocked me off balance, and all of the puddles kept sucking me in. By the time I reached the back of the church, the water was squishing in my sneakers, and my jeans were plastered to my skin. *What was I thinking wearing long pants anyway? I should have put on my swim trunks!* There was no sign of Dinah as I checked the back door. It was locked all right. My first thought was that she would be at our tree waiting for me. *She doesn't know I know she's locked out. Only a fool would stand under a tree in a storm. A tree's an even bigger lightning rod than an umbrella. Where could Dinah be?*

Then I remembered she'd spent several nights in the park by the YMCA. *Maybe she's in that playhouse. Is the playhouse any safer than under a tree? At least it's out of the rain.* The church was less than a mile from the YMCA on foot. I ran most of the way, only this time I stayed on the trails. By the time I reached the park, the rain had let up. The play area included a big wooden ship that was two stories high on one end and a playhouse that was three stories high at the other end. Mark and I called the playhouse the castle. There were all kinds of slides and tires and monkey bars in between. Depending on which way you went up, there was a swinging wooden bridge leading up to the castle.

I bounded up two stairs at a time and crossed the bridge to the castle. That put me up high enough to see into the second floor as I approached. "Dinah!" I called softly several times. No response. I didn't want to startle her by just walking right up. I think I was probably more worried about getting hurt myself if I surprised her than I was about scaring her.

I shined my flashlight in through the window and called, "Dinah!" again. Then I climbed inside, shining the flashlight up to the third floor. "Dinah! It's me, Matthew." Nothing. As I climbed the ladder to the top, tears started burning my eyes. Lucky I was dripping wet. No way I wanted Dinah to see my tears. But when I reached the top, Dinah wasn't there. I sat with my legs swinging over the ladder, heart pounding and eyes streaming. I buried my face in my hands.

Except for my sniffling, the only sound was the irregular drumming of water dripping off the roof of the castle onto the plastic slide down the other side. I didn't have any idea what time it was or where else Dinah might be. Since the storm had passed, I decided to walk to our tree to see if she might be there. I still had enough adrenaline pumping that I didn't realize how tired I was getting.

I kept a brisk, steady stride as I walked. *When Johnny comes marching home again, Hurrah! Hurrah! When Johnny comes marching home again, Hurrah! Hurrah! The ants go marching one by one, the little one stops to suck his thumb, and they all go marching down—to the ground—to get out—of the rain. Boom, boom, boom.* I didn't know all the words to *When Johnny Comes Marching Home*, so it kept turning into *The Ants Go Marching* in my head.

When I finally reached our tree behind the library, there was no one around. I walked along the edge of the creek to the bridge on the bike path. I leaned across the railing and listened to the rushing water. Still no sign of Dinah, and I was running out of ideas. I was also running out of steam. Part of me wanted to lie down right there on the bridge and go to sleep. I shined the flashlight down on my jeans and sneakers. In addition to being soaked, I was covered in mud and grass. I needed more than clean pajamas to get back into the house. I needed to wash up.

Since I already had the key to the church, I decided the best thing to do was walk back to the house, get my pajamas and a garbage bag out of the garage, and then walk back over to the church. At least I could run some water and get cleaned up without waking Mom and Dad. Yesterday I never would have considered walking from the church to my house in my pajamas, but tonight it made sense.

As I unlocked the back door of the church, I decided I'd better take my rain poncho, sneakers, and jeans off at the doorway so I wouldn't track water and mud through the church. I stuck them in my garbage bag and headed for the men's room upstairs. I was almost to the stairway at the other end of the basement when a flashlight popped on and blinded me. Oh, and I shrieked, too. That was when the other flashlight hit the floor. "Matthew? Is that you?"

"Dinah! I've been looking everywhere for you!" I cried. I completely forgot I wasn't wearing any pants. "I heard Dad tell Mom that he'd locked the door. How did you get in?"

Dinah picked up her flashlight, and we both shined our lights straight up, illuminating our faces without blinding each other. "When I couldn't get in the back door, I just came in through the bathroom window there by the nursery."

I was stunned. She'd been here in the church the whole time. "I can't believe you found an open window," I said.

"I didn't *find* an open window, Matthew," Dinah explained. "The very first night I stayed here I decided I better have a Plan B in case I got locked out. I checked all the windows in the church and chose that one to leave unlocked. It's got enough of a ledge on the outside that I could get in and out, and the blind is always closed on the inside, so nobody would notice that's it's unlocked."

I should have known that Dinah would be able to take care of herself. Suddenly, I remembered my pants were in my hand. I held the garbage bag in front of my groin. "Let me go get cleaned up," I said. I wished I had something more than my pajamas to put on. But even pajamas were better than standing there in my underwear another second.

It took forever to get all the mud off my legs and arms. I even had mud in my hair. I got the mud off of me and all over the bathroom. So I had to clean that mess up, too. When all of the mud was either down the drain or in my garbage bag, I put on my pajamas and gathered up all the used paper hand towels, stuffing them all the way to the bottom of the trash can.

Dinah was dressed and waiting for me when I returned. "Come on," she said. "I'll walk you home."

"You don't have to do that," I said. I was so tired by this time that I felt like a little kid. I didn't want to say so, but I was overjoyed that she was going to walk me home. Dinah took the garbage bag from me and pointed me toward the back door.

"You lead the way. I'll make sure the door doesn't lock behind us." Outside, she held my hand as we walked. "Thanks for looking for me, Matthew," she said. "You're the best friend I ever had."

❧ Sixteen ❧

MOM WAS SITTING on the edge of my bed feeling my forehead when I woke up the next morning. "Are you feeling okay?" she asked.

I stretched and rubbed my eyes. "I'm okay. What's wrong?" I asked.

"It's almost noon, honey," Mom said. "I just wanted to make sure that you weren't sick."

"Almost noon!" I scrambled out of bed and peeked out the window. Sure enough, the sun was straight up in the sky. Last night was all coming back to me. Dinah might be worried.

Mom laughed. "It's okay. Mark and Luke worked together and got your morning chores done. I've got lunch ready in the kitchen. I think you really are in the middle of a growing spurt."

I straightened my back and took a deep breath. "You think?" I asked, hoping it was true, but knowing that despite what my mom believed, I wasn't eating or sleeping any more than usual. Probably less.

"Hurry up and get dressed. I'll see you downstairs. I'm going to get your brothers started on pancakes and smoky links."

I smiled. My favorite breakfast. Mom occasionally made them for a Saturday brunch or Sunday evening meal, but I can't remember ever having that for lunch on a weekday.

By the time I got downstairs, Mark and Luke had roared through their first plate of pancakes. Mom handed me my plate and went back to the kitchen to get more for my brothers. I breathed in the delicious buttermilk steam hovering above them. "Pass the butter and syrup, please," I said to Luke.

When Mom came back with the pancakes for Mark and Luke, she turned to me. "Milk or juice?" she asked.

"Milk, please," I said. Nothing beats cold, creamy milk with pancakes.

Johnny was sitting in his high chair rolling his cut-up smoky link pieces around like marbles.

"Hey, Johnny, want some pancake?" I cut a small bite and raised it to his mouth with my fork.

"Cake!" he said, and gobbled it up. "More, more, more!" said Johnny, tapping his fists together.

I gave him several more bites while I devoured my smoky links.

By the time I was ready for more pancakes, Mark had finished his second plateful.

"May I please be excused?" Mark asked Mom.

"Yes, you may," Mom replied, putting two more hot cakes on my plate.

"Me, too!" cried Luke jumping up to follow Mark.

"You too, Luke," Mom replied.

When it was just Mom and Johnny and me, I worked up the courage to ask her something I'd been thinking about while I was wandering out in the rain last night. "Did you ever like anybody besides Dad?" *Anybody creepy? Or anybody named Jerry?* I stuffed a smoky link in my mouth to discourage her from asking me why I wanted to know.

Mom smiled as she thought about it. "Yes, there were a few," she said as she buttered her own pancakes and reached for the syrup. "Your dad and I didn't meet until college."

Johnny tapped his fists together again. "More cake!" Mom gave him a bite of hers.

"Did you ever think about marrying one of those guys—before you met Dad, I mean?"

"Oh, I think every girl has dreams of getting married as she's growing up, but I don't think I ever thought seriously about marrying any of those other boys," Mom said.

"Why not?"

"Well, it always seemed like the boys I really liked, really liked somebody else." Mom chuckled.

I took a big bite of pancake and pondered while I chewed. "Didn't any boys like you?"

"Oh, sure, there were boys who liked me, too," Mom said, giving Johnny another bite. "But for some reason I never seemed to like them as much as they liked me."

I chugged down the rest of my milk. "What about Dad? Did he have other girlfriends?"

"I happen to know of several girls who liked your dad when he asked me out."

"Really?"

"Sure," Mom said. "But your dad was always so focused on his own plans, I'm not sure he knew it." Johnny dropped his sippy cup of milk on the floor, and Mom reached down to get it. This was one of Johnny's favorite games. He threw the cup back on the floor. Mom played along.

"The first time your dad asked me out, he said, 'Theresa, God told me last night in a dream that I'm going to marry you. I was thinking we should go out on a date and see if He tells you the same thing.'"

"And did God tell you the same thing?"

"The same thing, but not right away. And not in the same way," Mom said. "It took me about two years of dating your dad before God just kind of whispered it in my heart. I might not have heard it if I hadn't given it enough time and listened closely." Mom put her fork down and rested her chin on her hand. "Even then, we both knew we needed to finish college first," she added. "Finish college first" was one of our family mottos.

"What if God hadn't told you or you hadn't listened?" I asked.

"I guess eventually God would have told your dad to marry someone else. But I'm glad I married your dad."

"Me, too," I nodded. "Do you think God will talk to me like that?"

"If you listen, God will talk to you," Mom said, "but it won't be the same way He talks to Daddy or to me.

God speaks to each of us differently. And I think you're already learning to listen."

❧ Seventeen ❧

IT WAS JUST after 1:00 when I arrived at our tree hoping to find Dinah. There was no sign of her as I approached, but when I circled the tree, I found a note stuck to the back of the tree trunk with pink bubble-gum. "M—Back @ 2—D." I thought about going inside the library, but with less than an hour, it didn't seem worth it. I pulled *The Last Battle* out of my book bag, stretched out under the tree and tried to pick up where I'd left off several weeks ago.

I hadn't read a page since I met Dinah. I rolled over on my stomach and kicked my feet up and down. I was looking at my book, but I was thinking about what would happen when Dinah's mom came back next week. Only one week left. One week from today.

Would her mom go back with Creepy Jerry? They just couldn't live there. They had to find someplace else. Someplace nearby. As my mind drifted to Dinah staying at the church, I felt another surge of brilliance.

Mrs. Miller needed someone to live in her guesthouse and help her out. Anybody could do that. Dinah and her mom needed a place to live. Dinah's mom may be a little crazy still, but then Mrs. Miller was pretty crazy, too. All I needed to do was find out a little bit more about Dinah's mom and then convince my dad to hire her!

That would be so perfect! Dinah and her mom could bring Mrs. Miller to church on Sundays and Wednesday nights. Why, if Mrs. Miller had Dinah and her mom sitting on each side of her, she wouldn't need her dogs. That would definitely make my dad happy! I felt myself getting caught up in the excitement. My mom and Kyle's mom could home school Dinah, too.

My mind got stuck on the thought of Kyle. Kyle would be back in August. *What if Dinah doesn't like Kyle? What if she likes him better than me? What if Kyle likes Dinah better than me?* I rolled over in the grass and tried to push the questions out of my head. We'd be like the three musketeers—all for one and one for all. Anyway, three's better than two. What does it say in Ecclesiastes? A cord of three strands is not quickly broken. I was so wrapped up in my thoughts, I didn't even notice Dinah walking up.

"Hey, Matthew," Dinah said as she sat down next to me. "Listen to this." She started playing a sweet, bluesy melody. It took me a minute, but I recognized the tune, *What a Wonderful World.* When she finished Dinah started dancing around. "I did it! I did it! That was in G. I can finally play a song cross-harp!"

"That was great!" I said. Dinah's eyes gleamed as she played the chorus again.

"It does kind of make me hyperventilate, though," she said. "I still need lots of practice. I just wish Steve could hear me!" Dinah played another little blues riff.

"Who's Steve?" I asked.

"Steve's the one who gave me the harp," Dinah said. "He used to play in a band at the Blues Basement where my mom was a waitress. He'd sit back in the kitchen with me after rehearsal and between sets. He let me play his G harp with him while he played cross-harp on the C."

"Was he your mom's boyfriend?" I asked. He sounded better than Creepy Jerry.

"I wish," Dinah sighed. "He was the nicest guy I ever met."

"So what," I persisted, "your mom just didn't like him?"

"Mom liked him all right." Dinah paused as she looked at me. "Mom and Steve were just friends . . . because . . . well, because he had a boyfriend."

"You mean because your mom had a boyfriend," I corrected her.

Dinah shook her head. "Mom's boyfriends come and go. I mean Steve had a real boyfriend."

"Oh." I felt my stomach knotting up. It was like Dinah was waiting for me to say something, only I really didn't know what to say. The first thing that popped into my head was something I'd heard Kyle say that made everybody laugh. "God created Adam and Eve, not Adam and Steve!"

All traces of Dinah's smile vanished from her face, and she just stared at me. I suddenly realized how easy it would be for her to beat me up.

"I'm sorry," I whispered. "I was just trying to be funny. I didn't mean to make you mad."

Dinah's shoulders dropped, and she just kept looking at me. "Don't you think God made Steve, too?" Dinah finally asked, her voice barely above a whisper. I watched as tears began pouring out the corners of her eyes. I could feel my eyes filling up with my own tears. I blinked to keep them back. I was afraid to say anything now—afraid whatever I said would only make it worse. I hung my head. Dinah still wasn't saying anything. Tears rolled down her cheeks. She really was waiting for me to answer.

"God made all of us," I told her. "I don't know why he made me so stupid, though." I looked at her, silently begging her to forgive me.

Dinah lifted the bottom of her t-shirt up to wipe her tears. "Matthew," she said sniffling a little, "you're the smartest person I ever met." She smiled, and I could finally breathe again. *Maybe even smart people say dumb things sometimes.*

❧ Eighteen ❧

WHEN I WENT to meet Dinah behind the library on Saturday morning, I was anxious to talk to her about her mom. I'd been thinking more about them living at Mrs. Miller's place, and I was hoping Dinah would be excited, too. We only had six days left.

Dinah was perched up in the tree chomping on a raisin bagel. I dropped my backpack next to hers beside the tree and climbed up across from her. As the branches became more familiar, I was getting a little faster and feeling a lot more comfortable. "Want half a bagel?" Dinah offered.

"No, thanks," I said. "Dinah, I've been thinking about what's going to happen when your mom gets back."

"She'll get a job, dump Jerry, and we'll find a new place to live," Dinah said shrugging her shoulders.

"What if I told you I think I found a job for your mom and a new place for you to live?"

Dinah stopped chewing. "What kind of a job?"

"All your mom would have to do is take care of an old lady who goes to our church. Just be her personal assistant. You know, like drive her around and do her shopping. Stuff like that. She's got a guesthouse right there beside her home where she wants her personal assistant to live." I climbed up a branch higher. "What do you think?"

Dinah shook her head. "I don't know if Mom's going to be able to drive." Dinah jumped out of the tree. I climbed back down and over to where she'd been sitting. I thought all parents could drive. *Do they take your license away if they think you're crazy? Maybe she just doesn't have a car.*

"Your mom wouldn't need a car. Mrs. Miller has at least three cars that I've seen." I said before swinging around and dropping to the ground.

"She needs more than a car," Dinah said and shook her head again. "She needs a driver's license." Dinah was rummaging through her backpack, but she didn't look like she was looking for anything in particular.

"My dad could help her," I said. "He's helped other people get their licenses."

"I don't think so," Dinah said. "Thanks anyway."

I was crushed. And I just couldn't understand why Dinah wasn't giving my idea a chance. "Mrs. Miller wants my dad to interview and hire the person. After your mom gets back, I can talk to my dad. He's always helping people. He'd want to help your mom."

"Let's go down to the creek." Dinah was still shaking her head. "I guess it's time I told you about my mom."

I felt a rush of adrenaline as I walked with Dinah to the creek. Her pace was slow, and I tried not to rush her. *She's going to tell me about her mom. Just listen. Don't ask any questions. Don't interrupt. Let her say everything she has to say before you say a word. And don't say anything stupid!*

She took her shoes off at the creek and waded into the water. I kicked my shoes off and followed. I picked a sunny spot to enter and watched little fish and tadpoles dart away. The cool water covered my feet and ankles. Smooth rocks massaged the soles of my feet near the bank. As I moved toward the middle, the water rose to my knees and the rocks changed to sand and then muck. I liked how the muck sucked my feet in and held on each time I took a step.

Dinah was doing her own muck stomp, back and forth like a rocking horse. She turned to face me, and I rocked back and forth, too. "A horse! A horse! My kingdom for a horse!" I called.

"What's that supposed to mean?" asked Dinah.

"I don't know," I shrugged. "My dad says it's Shakespeare."

Dinah lifted her right foot up out of the water and held it out between us. Thick black muck covered her toes and clung to the top of her foot. "Eeooooowah!" Dinah laughed, plopping her foot back into the water to keep from losing her balance.

I curled my toes into the muck and shifted my weight back and forth before bringing one of my muck-covered feet to the surface. First one and then the other. We stirred up enough muck that we couldn't see anything in the water around us.

Just when I thought she'd decided not to tell me about her mom after all, Dinah turned to me and said, "My mom's in jail."

"In jail?" I heard myself say. *Don't say anything stupid. Don't say anything stupid.* I mean, I knew people went to jail all the time, but not people I knew. Jail was for criminals—really bad people. How could Dinah's mother be a criminal?

"She was driving without a license, and the judge gave her sixty days, but she only has to do 30 days as long as she doesn't cause any trouble while she's there."

"I didn't know they put people in jail for that," I said.

"Usually they don't," Dinah explained, "but she was already on probation, so they violated her."

They violated her! Visions of police officers forcing themselves on Dinah's mother flashed through my mind. Anger shook my whole body as I cried out, "They can't do that! It's against the law! They can't just go around violating women!"

"Matthew," Dinah put her hands on my shoulders. "What are you talking about? They violated her probation and sent her to jail for a month for screwing up while she was on probation. Get it?"

It was slowly sinking in. Embarrassment rushed in as the anger drained out. "So why was she on probation?"

"Jerry," Dinah said with disgust. "He's the one who got her drunk and made her drive him around to begin with, and he's the one who made her drive his car to the store when the taillight was out. He's such a loser!" She started swishing her feet in the water and moving toward the bank.

We sat on the bank in silence and splashed our feet around in the water until the muck was all off. *Dinah's right. Dad's not going to hire someone just getting out of jail who can't drive. Dinah's mom will get out, and I'll never see her again.* We wiped our feet in the grass and put our shoes back on.

"Do you have an e-mail address?" Dinah asked me.

"No," I said. "Mrs. Cleary said I have to be 13 to get one."

"You don't actually have to *be* 13," Dinah said. "You just have to put down that your birthday was at least 13 years ago when you register."

"So do you have an e-mail address?" I asked.

"I just signed up for one last night," Dinah said. "I'm BluesHarpDiva@yahoo.com. But I need somebody to e-mail back and forth with. I was thinking we could get you an e-mail address, too."

"That'd be great!" I said. There were lots of computers in the library, but I never signed up for them. I always just read books. But I could get on a computer whenever I wanted.

"Once we have you signed up, there's something else I want to show you, too," Dinah said. "Let's go inside and see if we can get on a computer."

"What about Mrs. Cleary?" I asked.

"I'll go first," Dinah said. "You wait ten minutes. If I'm not back by then that means the coast is clear and there's a computer available. If not, then I'll be right back. Okay?"

"Okay," I replied.

Dinah crossed her fingers and held them up. "See you inside," she said.

❧ Nineteen ❧

I WAITED TEN minutes and then went in to the computer room. Dinah was on the farthest computer away from the door and back in a corner. "Pull up a chair," she said. I grabbed a chair as Dinah pulled up the Yahoo registration page. "What do you want to call yourself?"

"How about pianist@yahoo.com?" I suggested.

"We can try it," Dinah frowned as she checked to see if it was available. "Nope. You need to personalize it more—but don't use your real name."

"How about PKpianist?" I asked.

Dinah nodded. "That's better," she said. "What's the PK stand for?"

"Preacher's Kid," I said.

"PKpianist@yahoo.com is available! All right!" Dinah said. "Here, trade me places and fill out the registration." We switched chairs. "Make sure your birthday's at least 13 years ago, and only fill in the boxes with asterisks."

I filled out the form, picked my password, and in seconds I had my own e-mail account. I felt a little guilty because Dad always said that letting kids surf the web was like letting them drive all around the world unsupervised. I doubted that Mom agreed, but she never said so to me. One time I overheard Dad telling her, "When he's old enough to drive safely, he'll be old enough to use the Internet safely." They changed the subject as soon as they realized I was there, though. Fortunately, they never actually told me I wasn't allowed to use the Internet.

"Okay, now send me an e-mail so I for sure have your address," Dinah instructed. "Then I'll send you one back so you'll for sure have mine."

"Do you want me to write you a message right now?" I asked.

"No, just put 'test' as the subject and 'test' in the message part," Dinah said. "Then I'll reply back."

As soon as I sent the test e-mail, we traded places again. "Okay, here's how you get to the login page." Dinah switched back and forth between the mouse and the keyboard, but it didn't look that hard. "Now, you just enter your user name and password like this, and there—you're in! See, I've got the test message from you."

"Wow! That was fast," I said.

"Now I just click on reply, type in my return message, and click send," Dinah said as she replied to my test message. "All done. Now we can always e-mail back and forth."

"Thanks, Dinah," I said. *She's not just going to disappear at the end of the week.*

"Now, let me show you what I found surfing the net last night." Dinah pulled up a webpage with a NASA logo at the top. I read "Ask an Astrophysicist" across the middle of the page. "You can e-mail a question to an astrophysicist at NASA. What do you think?"

I was stunned. There was tons of information at my fingertips, and if I couldn't find the answer there, I could e-mail a real, live astrophysicist! "This is incredible," I whispered. It was like Dinah just gave me my own rocket ship and I could travel anywhere in the universe I wanted to go. I clicked on Relativity. Dinah watched as I scanned through all of the articles available on time dilation and space travel. "It doesn't look like anybody's asked my question," I said.

"So ask it," Dinah said.

As I scrolled down the form I had to tell them my age and grade level. Dinah was looking over my shoulder.

"Tell them you're 16 and a sophomore," Dinah suggested.

"Do you think it matters?" I wondered.

"Better they think you're a little older," Dinah assured me. "Plus, you're definitely at a high school level, right?"

"I guess." I typed in my new e-mail address along with my new age. I was so slow compared to Dinah. Finally, I pecked out my question, one key at a time:

The Bible says God is Light, and that 1,000 years on earth is like a day to God. If you assume God is traveling at the speed of light, and the planet earth is traveling at a constant speed through space, can you calculate a time dilation ratio, and would it be anywhere close to 1,000 years is like a day?

"What do you think?" I asked Dinah.

"Sounds good to me," she replied. "It says you could have an answer in a week or two. Let's see what happens."

Before we left, Dinah showed me how to close down the programs, get back onto the Internet and e-mail, and I saw that her test e-mail reply was there in my inbox. She also took me to Ask Jeeves and Google, so I could do more research on my own.

"The NASA website had gov at the end of the website address," Dinah told me. "That's good. Anything that's gov is from the government, and if it's edu it's from a school or university. Those are supposed to have the most reliable information."

"Which ones aren't reliable?" I asked.

"Anybody can put up a .com or .net website and put anything on it they want," Dinah replied. "You wouldn't believe some of the freaks out there. Surf around a little and you'll see."

❧ Twenty ❧

MARK WAS PLAYING baseball that afternoon at the ball diamonds by the YMCA. When I told Dinah my whole family would be there, she decided she could probably show up without anyone noticing and see my family.

"Mark plays shortstop for the Reds. He's number 8," I said. "Depending on how the game's going, my dad may be up walking around. Luke will want to follow him. Mom will probably have Johnny in a stroller."

"Don't worry, Matthew," Dinah said. "I've seen the photo of your family in your dad's office at church. I'll recognize them."

Sure enough, I saw Dinah standing by the bleachers for the opposing team during the first inning of Mark's game. Mark was the lead-off batter for the Reds. He opened the second inning with a stand-up double. By the bottom of the second inning, Johnny was getting restless, so I offered to take him for a walk in the stroller.

"Don't go too far," Mom said.

"Okay, Mom," I told her. "I'll stay on the walking paths between here and the library."

"Thanks, Matthew," Mom said as I turned the stroller toward the paths. "His wafers and fruit snacks are in the stroller. If he gets thirsty, just give him some water from his sippy cup."

I stopped behind the concession stand, outside my mother's line of vision and waited to see if Dinah might come over. I didn't have to wait long.

"Your brother's so cute!" she cooed. Johnny was pointing to the concession stand saying, "Candy, candy!"

"I have your candy, Johnny," I said, pulling out some fruit snacks and handing one to him. "We're going for a walk," I told Dinah. "Do you want to meet behind the library in about ten minutes?"

"That'd be great," Dinah waved to Johnny. "Bye-bye!"

"Bye-bye!" gurgled Johnny as he munched on his fruit snack. Juicy slobber dribbled down his chin.

Dinah was waiting for us when we rolled up to the tree. When I stopped the stroller, Johnny yelled, "Johnny run! Out! Run!"

"I think he wants out of the stroller," Dinah said.

"I think you're right," I agreed.

"Out! Out!" insisted Johnny. He pounded on the tray in front of him with his open palms.

I lifted Johnny out of the stroller and pulled out his favorite blue ball. It was just big enough that he had to use both hands to carry it. He picked it up and started running in circles around the stroller.

"How can he do that without getting dizzy?" Dinah asked. Then Johnny dropped the ball, accidentally kicked it toward the tree, and rolled over the top of it trying to pick it back up. It didn't faze him, though. It was just a new game. He got up, rolled over the ball, landed on his back, laughed, and got back up again. Dinah and I kept him between us, and rolled the ball back toward him whenever he accidentally kicked it away.

"Mark's a pretty good ballplayer, isn't he?" Dinah asked as we played with Johnny.

"Definitely," I nodded.

"Don't you play?" Dinah asked.

"I did when I was Mark's age." I wrinkled my nose and forehead. "This is the first year I haven't."

Dinah paused. "I've been thinking I should have you cut my hair in the back." I was glad Dinah changed the subject, but stunned she thought I could cut her hair.

"I've never cut anybody's hair," I said. "I'm not sure I'd do a very good job."

"I can do the front and sides myself," Dinah said, "but I can't see in the back. You can at least see what you're doing."

"I'll try if you want me to," I said. "You'll tell me what to do, right?"

"Definitely," said Dinah. "I found a decent pair of scissors at the church. We can do it tomorrow afternoon before our jam session in the sanctuary."

I nodded. "Well, I'd better get Johnny back to the game so Mom doesn't worry," I said.

"Can I pick him up?" Dinah asked.

"Sure," I said. "Come here, Johnny. Give Dinah a hug."

Johnny put his arms in the air and toddled over to me. I picked him up and gave him a big hug. Then I rubbed my nose in his belly. Johnny laughed and grabbed my hair.

"Whoa, Johnny!" I cried. "Not the hair!"

I handed him over to Dinah, who was waiting with open arms. "That's Dinah," I said. "Give Dinah a big hug."

"Dinah," Johnny said, grabbing her around the neck. "Dinah, Dinah, Dinah."

Dinah laughed and snuggled Johnny around the neck. Then she propped him on her hip. "What are you going to tell your mom if she asks you who Dinah is?"

"I'll sing *Dinah, Won't You Blow Your Horn* all the way back to the ball diamond," I said taking Johnny from her and hooking him back in his stroller. "If she asks, I can tell her I was singing that song to him."

"Can I play it for him on my harp before you go?" Dinah asked.

"Sure," I said. "He'd love that."

Dinah pulled out her harmonica and started playing *I've Been Working on the Railroad*. When she got to the chorus, I sang along, rolling Johnny back and forth to the rhythm. "Dinah won't you blow, Dinah won't you blow, Dinah won't you blow your horn? Someone's in the kitchen with Dinah. Someone's in the kitchen I know. Someone's in the kitchen with Dinah strumming on the old banjo."

When we got to the "Fee Fi Fiddle-e-i-o" part, I stopped rolling Johnny and the two of us clapped. "Oh, banjo. Oh, banjo," sang Johnny. When Dinah was done playing, Johnny clapped again. "Again! Again!"

"Sorry, buddy," I said. "We gotta go."

"I'll see you at 3:00 tomorrow," said Dinah, as she waved goodbye. Johnny and I sang all the way back to the ballpark.

❧ Twenty-One ❧

JOHNNY WAITED UNTIL our Sunday lunch in between bites of macaroni casserole to start singing, "Dinah! Dinah!"

"Well, now there's a name we haven't discussed yet," said Dad. "I wonder where he came up with that."

"I'll get the baby book!" shouted Mark. He pushed his chair back, jumped up and ran off. His napkin landed just outside the dining room.

Every time somebody suggested a new name for the baby, we consulted the book of baby names to see what it meant. We never did that for Luke or Johnny, but I guess this time my parents knew they weren't going to name the new kid Acts.

"I was singing *Dinah, Won't You Blow Your Horn* to him yesterday," I laughed. It was a pretty weak laugh, though, so I cleared my throat and added, "Yesterday he was singing 'Oh, banjo.'"

"Oh, banjo," sang Johnny, bobbing his head up and down.

"What's it say?" called Luke as Mark handed the book to Mom.

"Dinah. Let me see. It says that it's Hebrew, and it means good judgment," read Mom.

"That's right," Dad nodded. "Dinah means judgment or judged. Comes right from Genesis. Dinah was Jacob's only daughter."

I took a big bite of casserole and waited to see if Dad was going to go into the whole Shechem story. He didn't. I guess circumcision and murder aren't exactly proper conversations at the table. I could tell he knew the story, though, and wasn't about to name any daughter of his Dinah. In a way, it would be kind of cool to have a sister named Dinah, but in another way, I kind of already felt like Dinah was my sister.

"I still like Joy for a girl," said Dad. "Everybody knows what Joy means without having to consult some book of names."

"Joy, Hope, Grace, Faith, Charity. I don't know," said Mom. "I like Katherine with a 'K' and call her 'Katie.'" Mom flipped through the pages of the book. "Katherine means 'pure,'" she added.

"I think Dinah after a train is pretty cool," said Mark.

"Yeah," chimed in Luke. "Trains are cool."

"Dinah!" chanted Johnny, drumming his tray.

"What do you think, Matthew?" asked Dad.

"I like Katherine Joy," I said. "And we could call her Katie."

Mom looked from me to Dad and beamed. "Katherine Joy. Pure Joy!"

Dad changed the subject. "So, who's coming with me to watch the fireworks tonight?" he asked, looking around the table.

"I am," I said as Mark and Luke shouted, "Me! Me!" in unison.

"What do you think, Theresa?" Dad asked, turning back to Mom.

"I think I'll pack you a blanket and some bug spray so you can all watch from the field by the park," Mom replied. "They won't start until at least 9:30, so Johnny and I will have to pass."

There was a country club and golf course not far from the park where they set off great fireworks for the 4th of July. Dad, Mark, Luke and I had gone last year. We'd taken a blanket, but had to borrow bug spray from Kyle's mom. *I wonder if Kyle's going to get to see any fireworks tonight. Maybe I could slip away and watch the fireworks with Dinah.* I started plotting different excuses to get away from Dad and a fool-proof plan to convince Dinah to meet me there.

ও Twenty-Two ও

DINAH WAS WAITING for me with scissors and mirror in hand when I got to the church. I could tell that she'd already done the front and sides, and she looked like she had a plan for the back, too.

"Where'd you get the mirror?" I asked.

"Half of your neighborhood had garage sales last weekend," Dinah said. "Afterwards the trash dumpsters were like gold mines. I got this mirror, some jewelry and a whole new outfit to wear on Friday when I see my mom. That's what got me thinking about a haircut," she confided.

I thought Dinah's hair was pretty short already, so I never thought about her needing a haircut. The back was still real uneven, though. When I thought about it last night I figured I couldn't make it much worse.

"So, who usually cuts your hair?" I asked.

"I do, only I never cut the back until last month. Last time Mom saw me my hair was down to here," she said, pointing to the middle of her back. "Come on." She led me up to the bathroom beside the nursery. She already had wet paper towels spread out all around a chair.

"So why'd you cut the back?" I asked as she settled into her chair and handed me the scissors.

"Lots of reasons," Dinah answered. "It was hot and hard to keep clean, especially without knowing when and where I'd be able to wash it. But mostly I guess it was so I'd look more like a boy and people would leave me alone." She held up the mirror to one side. "Move over a little so I can see the reflection in the mirror behind you."

I moved over. "How's that?"

"Better," Dinah said. "Now, don't just cut it straight across the back. I want you to start right behind my ear lobes and kind of curve it gently in. Leave as much length as you can."

"Like this?" I said, running my finger from her earlobe, across the back of her neck, up to her other earlobe. She had little metal posts surrounded by a plastic circle on the backs of each ear. I looked up at her reflection in the mirror. For the first time since I'd met her, little gold balls filled the holes in her earlobes.

"Not quite that curvy," Dinah said. "Here. Give me back the scissors, and I'll show you." She picked up one of the wet paper towels and cut it into the shape she wanted. I held it up to the back of her head.

"Like that?" I asked.

"Can you get it any lower?" asked Dinah.

"How about like that?" I asked, dropping it another quarter of an inch.

"That's better," Dinah nodded.

"Don't nod!" I ordered. "Just hold real still." I pressed the pattern up against the back of Dinah's head with my left hand, and carefully cut along the bottom of it using the scissors in my right hand. Hairs of all different lengths fell to the floor, but most of them were sticking to the wet paper towels. When I was done, I used the pattern to brush off some of the little hairs on Dinah's neck. "How's that?" I asked.

Dinah moved the mirror around and turned her head from side to side.

"Hey! That looks pretty good!" Dinah said as she admired my work. "There's still that missing chunk, though." I could see that there was a handful of hair that was shorter on the left side. "Do you think you could just kind of cut some hair here and there to make that blend in a little more?"

"How do I do that?" I asked.

"Here. Take this comb and run it up through the back of my hair like this." Dinah used the comb to pull out the sides of her hair. "Then when I say stop, you stop moving the comb and snip off whatever hair is sticking out toward you. Okay?"

I had my doubts. "If you say so." I took the comb and started combing all of the hair in the back of her head up.

"Don't cut off more than a quarter of an inch at a time," Dinah instructed me. "You can always cut more, but you can't put it back."

Dinah continued guiding me until she was satisfied with the way the back of her hair looked. "That's great, Matthew!"

By the time we were done, we both had little light brown hairs all over us. When she stood up, she turned around and gave me a big hug. I still had the scissors in one hand and the comb in the other, but I hugged her back with my arms. I was surprised by how sweet her neck smelled. Not like perfume or soap. More like a banana on the one perfect day when it's not too green and not too brown. I could have stood there forever.

"Let's get this mess cleaned up," Dinah finally said when she let go. We picked up the paper towels being careful to keep the hair on them and stuffed them into a plastic bag.

As we worked, I found myself wondering about what she'd said. "You think people are less likely to mess with you if you look like a boy?" I finally asked her.

"Definitely," Dinah said, grabbing two clean paper towels off the stack by the sink.

"How come?" I asked. Dinah was getting the clean towels wet. She handed one to me and then started wiping the rest of the hair off the linoleum floor with the other one.

"That first night I left Jerry's I spent the night in a park downtown. I heard sirens several times through the night, and there were a lot more police cars driving around than what you see around here. I really didn't want the police to see me. And there were other people in the park, too. Mostly men. Some pretty scary women, too. And some boys. The boys all walked around like nobody better mess with them. I ended up hiding in the trees where no one could see me. I finally fell asleep."

I took my paper towel and started wiping up the linoleum, too. "So then what happened?" I asked.

"As soon as the downtown library opened, I went in and spent most of the morning wandering around between shelves looking at books, trying to figure out what to do. All of a sudden I noticed this guy behind me in the aisle, looking real intent like he was searching for a book. I went to another shelf and pretty soon that same guy was on the other side on his knees, pawing around the books there. I went to the other end of the shelf, and it wasn't long before the guy was looking at me through the books on the bottom shelf. No matter where I went, he'd show up on the other side of the shelf."

"So he was just watching you?" I asked.

"At first. Then he started wagging his tongue at me. It was so gross. I grabbed a book and sat down at a table near the help desk. Pretty soon he walked by and said something totally sick. I just stayed right there where a librarian could see me, hoping he'd leave. He walked by several more times and kept saying really nasty stuff. He'd say it really quick under his breath with his mouth barely moving, so no one else would notice."

"What did he look like?" I wondered if he'd ever been in our library.

"He was really tall with short dark hair, and he was breathing really heavy, like he had a massive sinus infection or something. He was old enough to be my father, maybe even a grandfather." Dinah shuddered. "He was just totally dirty with a big ol' beer belly hanging out of his filthy gray t-shirt."

"Did you tell the librarian?" I stuffed my wet paper towel in the bag and motioned for Dinah to hand me hers to stuff in the bag.

"No way," Dinah frowned. "I waited for like an hour after the last time he walked by me. Then I went to the kid's floor, grabbed a pair of safety scissors off one of the activity tables and went into the bathroom and cut off all my hair. Then I got out of there. I just started walking as far away from downtown as I could get." Dinah took the scissors and comb over to the sink and rinsed them off. When she was done she washed her hands and rinsed the sink.

"And you ended up out here?" I asked, picking up the scissors and comb and drying them off with another paper towel.

Dinah shook her head. "The next night I ended up in the barn with the farting cows. That was no good. So then I walked back this way and found the park over by the YMCA." Dinah put the last of the paper towels into the plastic bag and tied it shut. "I'll throw this away in the park later," she said. "Let's go play some music before it's too late."

❧ Twenty-Three ❧

As we walked into the sanctuary, I said, "Speaking of going to the park later, there'll be tons of people at the park around 9:30 tonight to watch the fireworks."

"I love fireworks!" Dinah said. "I was thinking I'd have to walk all the way downtown to see some tonight."

"The country club has great fireworks," I told her. "My dad and Mark and Luke and I will be sitting on a blanket in the park to watch them."

"What about your mom and Johnny?" Dinah asked. I liked the way she smiled when she said Johnny's name.

I shook my head. "Too late for Johnny. I was thinking we might be able to hook up in the crowd and watch them together."

"What about your dad?" Dinah asked.

"I could tell him that I have to go to the bathroom," I schemed. "As long as Mark and Luke didn't say they have to go, too, he'd let me go alone. Then I could meet you by the ship. The top of the ship would be a perfect place to watch the fireworks."

"Sounds like a plan," nodded Dinah. "And if you don't show, I'll know you couldn't get away. Either way, I'll get to watch the fireworks!" Dinah skipped along beside me. She pulled out her harmonica and started playing that John Phillips Sousa march that I don't know the name of, but I started singing, "Be kind to your web-footed friend, for a duck may be somebody's mother . . ."

We started marching up and down the aisles of the sanctuary as Dinah played. Dinah led the march, and I followed behind, pretending to play the piccolo. All at once Dinah sang, "You may think that this is the end. And it is!" She stopped marching so suddenly that I plowed right into her, knocking her onto the steps of the altar. There she was on her hands and knees, harmonica in hand, laughing. She turned around and sat on the steps. I sat down beside her.

"I like to come in here at night," Dinah said. "I sit right there in the middle of the aisle and play my harp in the dark." Dinah pointed down the center aisle. "Every night I want to light those candles up in front there, but I know I better not." We both stared at the long white candles in candelabras on either side of the pulpit. "Do you ever light those candles?"

I nodded. "Kyle and I were acolytes last year. Every Sunday morning at the beginning of the church service we'd walk down the aisle and light the candles. Then at the end of the service we'd put the little brass bell end of the lighter over them to put them out."

Dinah stood up and walked over to the pulpit. Compared to my dad, she looked awful small standing behind it. "Do you want to hear my candle poem?" she asked.

"Sure," I said, taking a seat on the front pew.

Dinah stood tall. Her eyes swept the sanctuary. I felt swallowed up in a crowd. Like the church was packed. Dinah rested her hands on either side of the pulpit and began reciting her poem:

Light me a candle
Breathe a prayer for me
Lend me a flicker of hope
That I might be able to see

Light me a candle
Brightness is what I need
I would gladly follow
If you would only lead

Light me a candle
For this moment may quickly pass
But don't let my moment of truth
Cast a shadow on anyone else

"How do you come up with all those poems?" I asked her.

"I don't know," Dinah replied. She came back around the pulpit. "They usually start with a feeling. Then I play my harp a little, and eventually the words just come."

"Will you e-mail me your poems as you write them?" I asked, thinking I'd probably have a whole book of poems by the end of the year.

Dinah looked at me intently and then smiled. "Sure," she said. "But right now I want to hear you play piano. I don't know when I'll have the chance to hear you again."

I nodded as I stood up and walked over to the piano bench. I lifted the lid and pulled out the classical music book.

"Play the hymns, Matthew," Dinah requested. "I like the songs you pick from the hymn book."

I pulled out the hymnal and began playing *The Love of God*, expecting Dinah to play along, but she didn't. She walked down to the center of the aisle, sat down, and just watched me. Since Dinah was just listening, I played songs in other keys, too. I played *Amazing Grace* in G, and *My Jesus I Love Thee* in D. I played all of my favorite hymns. When I got to *It Is Well With My Soul* in C, Dinah asked, "Is that in C?" I nodded. She pulled out her harmonica and played along.

Suddenly, I felt tears in my eyes. I realized this really was our last Sunday together in the sanctuary. Our sanctuary. I'd never be able to set foot in this sanctuary again without feeling Dinah in my heart.

We sat in silence for a long moment after we finished the song. "It's 5:00, Matthew," Dinah said softly. "You gotta go."

I nodded as I closed the hymnal and put it back in the piano bench. "So I'll see you at the fireworks," I said, holding up my crossed fingers.

Dinah crossed her fingers and held them up, too. "At the fireworks," she agreed. "And then again tomorrow by our tree. I'll be there by noon."

෨ Twenty-Four ෨

DAD PICKED A spot right in the middle of the field to spread out our blanket. Dad sprayed us all with bug spray and had me spray his back for him before we sat down. As we waited for the fireworks to begin, Mark gave us his play-by-play of yesterday's tourney, emphasizing all of his spectacular plays, followed by his analysis on why his team lost in the championship game. I waited about ten minutes.

"Dad, I gotta go," I said, wincing a little to make it look urgent.

"Matthew," Dad frowned. "I thought your mother told you all to go before we left."

"She did," I replied. "And I did. Now I have to go again. I must've drank a gallon of water this afternoon." I stood up to leave.

"I gotta go, too," said Luke jumping up to go with me. I couldn't believe it. Luke never wanted to leave Mark behind and go with me.

"What about you, Mark?" Dad asked.

"Nope," Mark said sprawling himself across all the extra room on the blanket. "I went. I'm good."

I weighed my options. Luke wasn't as safe as Johnny, but I'd rather see Dinah with Luke along than not see her at all. Luke didn't have to know Dinah was my friend.

"I'll take him to the port-a-potties over by the playground," I said, taking Luke by the hand. "Come on, buddy."

There were people lined up waiting outside all four of the johns. "Hey, Luke," I said, "do you have to go real bad?"

"Nope," said Luke. "Not anymore."

"I have an idea," I said. "Let's go play on the ship until the lines are shorter and we have to go again."

"But I want to see the fireworks," Luke whined.

"We'll be able to see them from the top of the ship," I told him. "I'll be the captain, and you'll be my first mate, and we'll have to batten down the hatches and try to weather the terrible storm."

"Yeah!" shouted Luke, jumping up and down. He loved using his imagination. The only thing Mark ever imagined with him was sports. And Mark was always the hero. Sometimes Luke got to be on Mark's team and get an assist, but usually Luke was the poor pitcher who gave up a grand slam in the World Series or the unfortunate goalie who gave up a penalty kick in the World Cup.

As we jogged over to the ship I was priming Luke's imagination with sharks and whales and battles with pirate ships. Luke raced up to the top deck and ran smack into Dinah.

"Hey!" shouted Luke. "No girls on our ship!" Luke came running back to me. "Captain! Captain! There's a girl on our ship!"

"Hold on, mate!" I laughed and nodded at Dinah. "Girls aren't all bad. Maybe she's a Siren.

"Woooo, Woooo, Woooo!" Luke screeched like a siren.

"Not that kind of siren, mate!" I laughed. "The kind that sings songs or plays music. She might help keep our spirits up during all of our terrible battles and storms."

Luke didn't look convinced. "I'd be honored to be your Siren, sir." Dinah saluted us both. "You can call me Siren, okay?" Luke looked at Dinah and then back at me. I nodded.

"Okay, Siren," said Luke, "but we're gonna have a BIG storm, and we might have to throw you overboard, and you'll be swallowed by a BIG whale."

Dinah laughed. "Aye, aye, sir!"

"Okay, mate," I said to Luke, "you need to take the wheel and steer the ship while I stand on deck and watch for whales."

"Aye, aye, Captain," Luke mimicked Dinah.

"How old are you mate?" Dinah asked Luke.

"I'm five," Luke said, holding up five fingers, "and a half."

"Five and a half," said Dinah rubbing her chin. "That's definitely old enough to steer this ship." Luke took his place behind the captain's wheel, and Dinah and I went to the front of the deck.

"Sorry I had to bring Luke," I said.

"No problem," said Dinah, "especially if he thinks my name's Siren."

"Yeah, Johnny started singing 'Dinah' at lunch today. If Luke comes back saying we met a new friend named Dinah, my mom would definitely think something's up." Just then the first firecracker shot high in the air and burst into a red mushroom. "Battle stations!" I called to Luke.

"Battle stations!" cried Luke, jumping up and down and clapping his hands. He ran up and nestled himself between Dinah and me to watch the fireworks. Every time one skyrocketed into the air and exploded, Luke yelled, "Yeah!" and clapped, then he'd yell "Ooooo, green!" or "Oooh, purple!" or whatever colors showered down.

I liked watching the different colored lights on Dinah's face as much as the fireworks themselves. Her fair skin faintly reflected the rainbow of fireworks, and the sparkles danced in her eyes. I thought her hair looked pretty good, too. The whole show was shorter than I ever remembered, but the grand finale was the best ever. When it was over, I took Luke's hand. "Come on, mate. Better not keep Dad waiting."

"See ya," I said to Dinah as we turned to go.

"Noon," she answered, nodding.

When we got back Dad was folding the blanket. Mark said, "About time! What took you guys so long?"

"There was a line, so we went and played on the ship while we waited. Then when the fireworks started we just watched them from there."

"It was a terrible storm and a BIG battle!" shouted Luke.

"Sorry, Dad," I said. "We came back as fast as we could once the show was over."

Dad nodded. "Let's go home."

❧ Twenty-Five ❧

IT WAS AFTER 10:30 when I got to the library Monday morning. Dinah said she'd meet me at noon, so I went straight in and signed up for a computer. I knew it was too soon to hope for an answer from the astrophysicist, but I thought it would be a good idea to practice checking e-mail.

When I logged onto Yahoo I had *two* messages from Dinah—the test message and a new one from Saturday night." I opened the new message.

PK,

Thanks for letting me meet Johnny. Makes me wish I had a little brother. If I could pick a brother, tho, I'd pick you. I'm glad we have e-mail. Promise you'll write!

Love ya!

BHD

I clicked on reply.

BHD,

*Now you've met Johnny and Luke. You make a good Siren.
I promise I'll write. Remember you promised to send me all your
poems, too! See ya! PK*

I read over what I'd written. That was good for
now. I clicked "send," and the e-mail disappeared into
cyberspace. I logged out of Yahoo and checked the
time. I still had almost 20 minutes, so I went to Ask
Jeeves. I liked the idea that I could just ask him anything. I typed in "Is the baby a boy or girl?" and hit
enter. A bunch of websites popped up instantly with all
kinds of tests on whether the baby would be a boy or
girl.

The first one I tried required registration. I decided
I'd better not register. The second one had like 20
questions that I started answering, only I didn't know
what color my mom's urine was, when the baby was
conceived, or what she was craving. I started making
up answers, but gave up. Not like I'd believe it anyway.

Next I typed in "Will Dinah be okay?" That gave
me a bunch of blogs about people named Dinah. Not
my Dinah. This was really dumb. Then I realized I
could ask Jeeves the same question I asked the astrophysicist. I couldn't remember exactly how I'd asked

the question, so I typed in, "The Bible says that God is light and that a thousand years is like a day to God. Can you calculate the time dilation ratio between time on earth and time traveling at the speed of light?" and pressed enter.

A whole page of websites popped up. I clicked on the very first one, *Life Spectrum Hypothesis* and began reading about possible explanations for the nature, creation, and evolution of the DNA molecule and life. I scrolled down through formulas and scientific illustrations until I saw the following subject written in bold letters, "EINSTEIN'S RELATIVITY AND THE NEW TESTAMENT."

I couldn't believe it. It was all right there in front of me, including Einstein's time dilation formula and the conclusion that if God is traveling at 99.9999999999999% of the speed of light, then one day would equal 1,000 years! And there was more, too.

The website applied Einstein's formula that $E = mc^2$ to two different verses in the book of Matthew: that the faith of a mustard seed can move a mountain, and that if two people on earth agree about anything they ask for, God will do it. The substantial energy in moving a mountain is E, a small mass like a mustard seed is *m,* and two people agreeing are c^2. *Two people agreeing are like the speed of light squared. Two people agreeing are like God squared.* I'd really have to think about that one.

All of a sudden I remembered I was supposed to meet Dinah at noon. I scribbled down the website so I could come back and read more. I darted out of the computer room and almost crashed into Mrs. Cleary, who was walking by with a stack of books to reshelve. "Sorry, Mrs. Cleary!" I said, slowing to a brisk walk. As soon as I was out of the building, I dashed to our tree. Dinah was there waiting for me.

"You're not going to believe it!" I shouted, dumping my backpack on the ground by the tree and digging out my notebook.

"What?" Dinah asked, moving in closer to see what was in my bag.

"I asked Jeeves the same question we e-mailed the NASA astrophysicist, and the very first website that came up answered all of my questions and more!" I opened my notebook to the website and waved it around like I'd just found a million dollars.

"That's great, Matthew!" Dinah said, dodging the notebook as I flung it toward her face. When she took the notebook from me to see what I'd written, I grabbed the limb of the tree and was sitting on top of it in an instant. I loved this tree. A hundred years ago it was just one of those little propeller seeds, but today it was 100 feet tall. Its upper limbs extended to the heavens while the lower limbs embraced me.

"So where have you been all morning?" I asked, swinging my legs back and forth right beside her head. She stepped back and looked up at me.

"I was over at the mall," she said. "I've been wanting to check out all of the dumpsters on a Monday morning right before trash collection." She didn't sound very enthusiastic for someone who was just returning from a treasure hunt.

"What did you find?" I asked.

"Not as much as I was hoping," Dinah admitted. "There was so much food and sticky drink stuff all over everything. It was nasty."

"Let's have lunch." I shouted and jumped out of the tree. "I'm starved!" For the first time ever, I landed right on my feet. I took a deep breath and stretched out my limbs. Our tree's shade swallowed me up, shadow and all.

"All I've got is a bag of animal crackers and some apple juice boxes that just expired last week," Dinah said, putting down my notebook and rummaging through her own backpack.

"That's okay," I said. "I brought sandwiches and stuff for both of us. We'll save yours for dessert."

‹∂ Twenty-Six ∂›

THE REST OF the week was a total blur of emotions. On the one hand I was really excited about finding an answer to my question, plus answers to questions I hadn't even thought of yet. On the other hand, each day was one day closer to Dinah's leaving. She was "all jazzed" about seeing her mom, whatever that meant. I was trying to be happy for her.

Wednesday was the worst. It rained all day, so I was stuck at home. Mom was tired. Johnny was cranky. I finally finished reading *The Last Battle*. Luke followed Mark around all day until Mark decided to take a nap. Then he followed me around wanting to play pirates and whales. We pretended like we were shipwrecked. I took all of the money out of my Monopoly game and we took turns hiding it and discovering each other's buried treasure.

Dinah was in my brain all day long. I wondered where she would go to stay dry. Maybe she would just hang out inside the library. As long as I wasn't around, she might be okay. Plus she'd be back with her mom day after tomorrow. I looked all around the sanctuary during Wednesday night's service. No sign of her anywhere. I made sure the back door was unlocked after we put out the trash.

Everything was still pretty soggy on Thursday, but it wasn't raining, so Mom let me go to the library. I went straight to our tree. Dinah was propped up against it, flipping through the harmonica book.

She was waiting for me like a present under the tree. I suddenly wished our tree was a Christmas tree that stayed green all year round instead of a maple tree whose leaves would turn brilliant red only to fall down and die. I pictured Dinah wrapped in a winter coat waiting for me under the bare limbs. Only she wouldn't be there. And even when the leaves returned, Dinah wouldn't.

Dinah looked up at me. "Sorry I couldn't get here yesterday," I said.

"That's okay. I figured you'd be stuck at home with the rain and all."

The maple leaves still had drops of rainwater on them. Every now and then there'd be just enough breeze to rustle the leaves. Droplets fell on my face. I took a deep breath. The air smelled fresh and clean. This would still be a great place to hang out, even without Dinah. Not with Kyle or anybody else, though. For me alone.

"Here's the last library book," Dinah said, handing me the harmonica book. We both held the book together for a second before she slowly looked up into my eyes. Her fingers let go of the book. Her eyes said thank you without any words at all.

As I tucked the book into my backpack, Dinah said, "It's too wet to eat here today. Let's meet at the picnic tables back by the park. Around noon, okay?"

I nodded. We would meet at noon today. At noon tomorrow she would meet her mom at Jerry's. I opened my mouth to say something like, "Sure, let's meet at noon," but nothing came out. Dinah shifted her backpack from her shoulder to the middle of her back. "See ya then," she said. I watched until she disappeared into the woods. Then I closed my mouth.

I'd been thinking about all the books I was using in the library. Now that I had my formula, calculations, and proof, all I needed to do was go back through the books and pull out the supporting principles and explanations so that I really understood the proofs. I had to be able to explain it all to Mom and Dad and answer all of their questions, too. Dad would probably be more excited about the faith moving mountains part than he would about the time dilation stuff.

Before I settled in with the books, though, I wanted to check e-mail and see if the NASA astrophysicist would confirm what Jeeves gave me. I logged into Yahoo. There was nothing from the astrophysicist, but I had two new e-mails from Dinah. One was from yesterday, the other from Tuesday. I decided it would be better to read them chronologically and clicked on Tuesday's e-mail.

PK,

Thanks for the e-mail. I'll send you my poems as long as you keep writing back. I wrote this one last night.

Sometimes the rest of the world is asleep,
And I find that I'm all by myself.
I realize I'm not what I seem to be,
But neither is anyone else.

BHD

I pulled out my notebook and copied down the poem on the back page. Then I clicked on Wednesday's e-mail.

PK,

I guess the rain kept you in today. I missed you. I guess I'm really going to miss you next week. Here's another poem.

Being Invisible
Cold and Hungry
But not Freezing or Starving
Tired and Lonely
But not Exhausted or Depressed
Invisible, I am Invincible
But if you see me,
I may disappear forever.

I wrote that when I was still sleeping in the playhouse at the park. Hope it's sunny tomorrow so I can see you.

BHD

I copied that one down, too. Then clicked on reply.

BHD,

Thanks for the poems. Before I met you I thought this summer was going to totally suck. Instead it's been the best ever. I'm glad you're my friend. PK

I didn't even want to think about how much I was going to miss Dinah. Definitely more than I'd missed Kyle.

෬ Twenty-Seven ෬

WHEN I GOT to the park, Dinah had a huge picnic spread out for us on one of the tables.

"Wow!" I said pulling out the lunch I'd packed. "Where'd you get all this food?" There were black olives, cans of tuna, boxes of crackers, a can of Cheez Whiz, Pop Tarts, and a can of mandarin oranges.

"Today we get to clean out my food stash," laughed Dinah. "Look." She handed me two little glass jars filled with little red pieces of something. "I've been saving these for you. I couldn't believe it when I found them last week!"

"So what are they?" I asked.

"They're pimentos!" Dinah said. "Didn't you know they sell jars of pimentos without olives?"

I shook my head. "I've only seen them in olives." I popped open one of the jars, dug out a pimento, and popped it in my mouth. "Thanks," I said. It was pretty good, but it didn't taste the same apart from the olives. I offered some to Dinah and ate the rest of the jar. "Can I save the other jar for later?" I asked.

"Sure," said Dinah.

"Here," I said handing her my sack lunch. "You can have this for dinner, since we're cleaning out your stash."

"Thanks," said Dinah. "Want some soy milk?"

"Soy milk?" I asked, wrinkling my nose.

"Here, try some," said Dinah, pouring a little into a plastic cup for me. It looked like milk, only a little brownish. "It's even better cold." Dinah poured a cup for herself, too, and chugged it. "I found ten boxes of the stuff during my garage sale fest." She poured herself another glass. "It doesn't have to be refrigerated either. At least not until after it's opened. I've been drinking half a box warm at night before I go to sleep. Then I put the other half in the church fridge, and drink it the next morning." She chugged the second glass.

I held the plastic cup to my nose. It smelled more like dried leaves than milk. I took a sip and shrugged. It wasn't cold. It wasn't creamy. It definitely wasn't milk. "It's okay, I guess."

"That's what I thought on the first box," Dinah nodded. "Now that I'm on the last box, I'm hooked. I think I'm going to have cravings!" She picked up the box and started reading the nutritional facts from the side panel. "It's got lots of protein and calcium, and look at this." She held the box for me to see. "One cup of this stuff has half of the Vitamin B_{12} you need for a whole day."

"Let me see that," I said, taking the box. "Each box has six servings. You say you've had ten of these boxes?" Dinah nodded. "Well that's enough B_{12} to last you for the next month!" I calculated.

Dinah took the box back. "Well, it doesn't have any warnings, so it can't hurt me. Maybe I'm just making up for the last month!"

Next Dinah opened the tuna, put a little on a cracker, and squirted the Cheez Whiz on top. "Here you go," she said handing it to me.

I popped the whole thing in my mouth and chewed. "Not bad," I said as soon as my mouth was moist enough to talk again. I dug my sports bottle out of my backpack and took a big drink. As long as there was water, Dinah could have the soy milk.

We worked our way through Dinah's feast until I was as stuffed as a trash bag at Christmas. The sun was out now, and the grass wasn't quite so wet. Only the sidewalk was dry, though. I stretched out on my back on the warm cement, hands behind my head. I closed my eyes and wished that this moment would never end.

After a few minutes, I heard Dinah gathering up the trash. I got up to help her.

"I checked on MapQuest," Dinah said. "It's almost nine miles from the church to Jerry's house. I'll be out of the church by 7:00 tomorrow morning." She paused long enough that I thought she was waiting for me to say something. I didn't know what to say. If I said anything, it would probably be something stupid. Like, wouldn't you rather stay here hiding in our church than go back with your mom? Duh. If I tried to tell her how much I was going to miss her, I'd cry for sure. Just the thought pushed the tears out of my head and into my eyes. So I stood there with my hands in my pockets, staring at the ground.

"I'll make sure that I lock the door when I go," she said finally. I nodded. How could I be sad for me and happy for her at the same time? Dinah sat down at the picnic table and pulled out her harmonica. I recognized the song she was playing. It was the one everyone sings on New Year's Eve—the one they sing at the end of *It's A Wonderful Life*. Zuzu's little voice echoed in my head, "Teacher says that every time a bell rings, an angel gets his wings." *Auld Lang Syne*. That's the name of it, whatever that means. I'd have to look that up.

Dinah played one song after another. I stuffed my hands in my pockets and sat down beside her. I just listened. I knew as soon as I moved a muscle she'd be gone for good. Eventually she quit playing anyway. I watched her put her harmonica back into her backpack. She came over to where I was sitting and reached out. She put her hands on my wrists and pulled them out of my pockets. She held both of my hands in hers. "Matthew," she said. "It's after 2:00. What do you want to do?"

I shrugged my shoulders and felt tears flooding my eyes and running down my cheeks. *I want you to tell me when I'm going to see you again. I don't want to say goodbye until I know for sure when I'll see you again.* She gave me a hug, and that was it. I was totally bawling like a baby. I kept my mouth shut, though. A bawling baby was still better than a blubbering idiot. Dinah led me back over to the picnic table and sat me down. She took my face in her hands and said, "Let's throw this trash away and walk back to our tree. We can sit up in the tree until 3:00, then we'll have to go, okay?"

I nodded. She led me through the motions. Only I didn't climb the tree. I laid down in the shade and just watched her up in the tree. She was wearing those jean shorts, dirty-white jogging shoes, and an oversized black t-shirt exactly like the day I met her. *Hard to believe that's the same person I thought was so creepy the first time I saw her.* Now that Dinah was my friend, it was hard to imagine how I could have thought such weird stuff about her.

The ground beneath me was still damp, but I didn't care. I studied the grass around me. I'd never noticed how many tree roots there were. Like a secret maze that peeked through here and there. Or maybe little wooden iceberg tips hinting at what lay below. Were they all part of the same root or different roots criss-crossing underground? One thing for sure—they were all part of this same tree.

I tried to hold perfectly still, but it didn't slow down time. Before I knew it, it was 3:00. Time for me to get on my bike and ride home. Dinah led me to my bike. We walked in silence. She crossed her fingers and held them up. "I'll see you again soon," she said. I nodded. I crossed my fingers and held them up, too.

"Promise you'll write?" Dinah asked.

I nodded again. She gave me a quick hug and disappeared behind the library. What could I do? I got on my bike and rode home.

❧ Twenty-Eight ❧

I DIDN'T GO to the library at all on Friday. I went to the church and played piano for hours. I'd played just about every hymn I knew out of the hymnal when Dad came in and sat down on the front pew.

"You're becoming a fine pianist, Matthew," he said. "I'm proud of how hard you've studied and practiced this summer." The only time Dad ever used the word proud was when he talked about one of us kids. He'd tell Mark he was proud of him after a game. He'd tell Luke that he was proud of him when he put a puzzle together real fast. I couldn't remember the last time Dad told me he was proud of me, though.

I'd played out all of my emotions. All I felt was numb. It was a good thing, too. If he'd said that an hour ago, I'd have probably burst into tears. Try explaining that to your dad.

"Come here and have a seat," Dad motioned to the pew beside him. I closed up the hymnal, put it back in the piano bench, and went to sit by my dad. "How's your project coming along?" I took a deep breath and felt some of the excitement from all I'd learned rushing back into me.

"Good," I said. "I think you and Mom are going to be surprised when I present it to you next month."

"I'm looking forward to that," Dad smiled. "Do you have any questions or need any help to get it ready?"

I shook my head. "I don't think so. But if I do, I'll let you know."

Dad nodded.

"Has Mark asked you for help yet to calculate all of his averages and statistics?"

I shook my head again. "Nah, the season isn't over until the first week of August. He'll just be gathering his data until then. It may take him at least a week after that to realize he's going to have to do the math."

Dad laughed. "You're probably right." He stretched his arms out across the back of the pew, one behind me and one reaching all the way to the other end of the pew. "I love this sanctuary," he said. "God talks to me here. I hope he talks through me here, too."

I nodded. I decided to practice what I'd learned with Dinah and just be quiet when I didn't know what to say. It still felt a little awkward, but not near as bad as saying something stupid.

"You know in medieval times, sanctuary was more than just the holy place in the house of God where people gathered to worship."

"Really?" I asked. I shifted in my seat. My palms were getting sticky.

"That's right," Dad continued. "People who were in trouble with the law would seek sanctuary inside the church. As long as they were in the church, the king and his armies couldn't touch them."

I suddenly panicked. *Dad knows about Dinah! He knows that she stayed here in the church hiding from the child welfare. But she's gone now. She's back with her mom. There's nothing they can do now, is there?*

Dad kept right on talking. "In modern times, it's not the building that gives sanctuary, but the living Body of Christ. It's the members of the church together that have to join together and provide refuge to the least of those among us as well as to those members of greater means."

He's just working on another sermon! I let out a huge sigh of relief. Dad stopped. "I'm sorry, son," he said. "I didn't mean to preach to you. I guess preaching is a hard habit to break when I'm in this sanctuary."

"That's okay, Dad," I said.

"Anyway, I'm glad to see that you find peace here in the sanctuary by playing piano." Dad cleared his throat. That was a sure sign that he was going to change the subject and move on to what he really wanted to talk to me about. "You know, your mother was a little worried about you with Kyle being gone all summer and the new baby on the way and all."

"I'm okay, Dad," I said.

Dad nodded. "I know you are. I think your mother was about convinced, too, until this week with the rain all day Wednesday. She said you still weren't yourself last night or this morning."

"It has been kind of a long week," I agreed. He waited. I did, too. He broke the silence first.

"You know, it won't be long before the new baby's here," Dad said. "It could be a couple of weeks before we all get settled in and used to each other."

"I know, Dad," I nodded.

"But no matter how busy or crazy it gets you can always come find me, right?" Dad kind of pulled me toward him with the arm he had been resting behind my back.

"I know." I just kept nodding.

"Okay, Matthew," he said. "So is there anything else we need to talk about?"

I pushed Dinah out of my brain and tried to think of something else. I just needed to think of one thing to talk about and that would convince Dad we were good for at least another week or two. Then he could convince Mom.

"Do you think the baby's a boy or a girl?" I asked.

Dad laughed. "I've stopped trying to guess. I thought Luke was going to be a girl, and then when he wasn't, I was thoroughly convinced Johnny would be a girl." He stretched his arms back out and crossed his legs. "What do you think?"

"I think it's a girl," I said, leaning back and crossing my legs like Dad, only in the opposite direction.

"I guess we'll know soon enough," Dad said.

I nodded. "Do you know what Kyle calls the baby?" I asked. Dad shook his head. "He calls her Acts."

Dad nodded seriously. His eyes were smiling, but he pursed his lips and furrowed his brow. "Matthew, Mark, Luke, John, and Acts. Hmmm. It does have a ring to it, don't you think?"

We both laughed.

"I love you, Matthew," Dad said.

"I love you, too, Dad."

෬ Twenty-Nine ෬

THAT SUNDAY MORNING, just as Dad was getting into his sermon, it happened. We were in our usual pew, three rows back on the right side. Mom was in the middle. Luke and Mark were on her left; Johnny and I were on her right.

"Over the past few weeks, I've preached about God's holy temple, and how God is not a respecter of persons. Today, I want to talk to you about sanctuary."

Mom gave me this funny look. The more Dad talked about the church being a sanctuary, the more I had this feeling that Mom knew about Dinah. *How? How could she know?* I remembered her saying that God talks to each of us differently. *Maybe God somehow let her in on the secret.*

Mom gave me a reassuring glance. *She knows all right. She's waiting for me to tell her when I'm ready.*

Johnny started getting restless. Mom leaned over and whispered in my ear, "Could you hold him on your lap and see if he'll sit still?" I nodded and whispered to Johnny as I lifted him on my lap. He settled down, but it wasn't long before I heard some commotion coming from Luke and Mark on the other side of Mom.

I looked at Mom to see why she wasn't trying to quiet them down. She had an odd look on her face again. Her eyebrows were all wrinkled up, like she couldn't quite decide what to do. Finally, Mark whispered loud enough for me to hear what he was saying, "Just be quiet before you get us all in trouble!" That got Dad's attention, too. He frowned at Mark, but continued preaching.

Then the whole congregation heard Luke say, "But it's wet! Mom had uh accident!" Dad looked at Mom. Mom just grimaced.

Dad shot out of the pulpit, shouting, "Are you all right, Theresa?"

Barking erupted from behind me. Suddenly a black Labrador wearing a brown leather backpack bounded up the aisle toward Dad, leash trailing. Dad and the dog slammed into each other right by our pew. Dad grabbed the pew and managed to keep from falling.

That got the whole congregation on its feet. Everyone except Mom. It was like the Tower of Babel. I could hear all these people talking, but none of it made sense.

Then Mrs. Miller came hobbling up the aisle after the dog calling "King! King! Here boy! Heel! Heel!" A yapping collie with a pink backpack trotted along beside her.

Mark and Luke were whooping and hollering, which only excited the dogs more. Johnny was jumping up and down, too. "Doggie! Doggie!"

"Get these dog-suh away from my wi-fuh!" Dad snapped. He sounded exactly like Grandpa!

Jim Reed, a volunteer firefighter, sprang into action. He grabbed Tom Stone and Ben Arnold, and the three of them herded Mrs. Miller and her dogs away from my dad, back out of the sanctuary.

"Theresa! Are you all right?" Dad asked, moving into the pew in front of us.

Mom nodded. "I'm fine, dear, but I think my water just broke."

"The baby!" Dad shouted. "The baby's coming!"

Dr. Westin appeared beside me. "Would you mind if I have a seat here by your mom?" she asked. I took Johnny by the hand, and we scooted down the pew away from Mom. "Any contractions, Theresa?" she asked as she slipped her fingers around Mom's wrist to check her pulse. Dr. Westin was some kind of foot doctor. I seriously doubted she had ever delivered a baby, but I was glad she was there just the same.

"I've had some Braxton-Hicks contractions on and off all week," Mom told her. "I had a mild one just before my water broke."

"Okay, let me know if you have another one, and we'll start timing them." Mom nodded. "When are you due?"

"Next Friday, the 16th," Mom told her. Mom was taking deep breaths, but she looked like she was doing okay.

"Looks like you're not going to have to wait until then," Dr. Westin said, smiling.

Jim Reed's wife, Lois, made her way to the front and took Mark and Luke by the hand. Mrs. Reed was Luke's Sunday school teacher, and she'd had Mark and me before Luke. She called over to me, "Matthew, bring Johnny. You boys come with me." I looked at Mom, and she nodded. *Everything's going to be okay.*

"Now, don't you worry, Theresa," said Mrs. Reed. I'm going to take these boys back to your house and make sure they get some lunch. We'll just wait to hear from you."

"You wait here, Theresa," Dad said. "I'll run home and get the car to drive you to the hospital."

"My bag is packed at the foot of our bed," Mom told him.

Kyle's mom came running up holding a stack of towels from the nursery. "Here you go, Theresa." Dr. Westin took a towel and helped mop up around Mom.

Kyle's dad caught my dad before he could take off. "Come on, Paul. Let's get Theresa into our car, and I'll drive you both to the hospital."

Dad looked at Mom. Mom looked at Dr. Westin. Dr. Westin nodded, "I'll be happy to ride along if it makes you feel any better."

Dad reached in his pocket and turned to Kyle's mom. "Here are my car keys. Theresa's bag's all packed at the foot of our bed. We'll meet you at the hospital."

My brothers and I filed out the back of the church with Mrs. Reed. Mr. Reed was standing by Mrs. Miller, trying to get the dogs calmed down and into the car. "I understand," he was saying. "Let's just get you all home."

Mrs. Reed shook her head. "Strapping a little knapsack on a dog's back doesn't make it a service dog," she muttered. "You'd think they'd have sense enough not to let untrained dogs into the church!"

✑ Thirty ✑

IT WAS TUESDAY afternoon before things settled down
enough at our house for me to go to the library. I
hadn't been there since Thursday morning, the last day
I saw Dinah. I went directly to the computer room and
logged onto Yahoo. I had three new e-mails: two from
Dinah and one from the NASA astrophysicist.

Dinah sent one Thursday night before she left, and
another one yesterday afternoon. I opened the one
from yesterday.

Hey PK!

*I was kind of hoping I'd have an e-mail from you by now, but
I guess you've been busy. We're moving to Cincinnati tomorrow
morning. Mom has a friend with an apartment downtown. We'll
stay with her until we can afford a place of our own. Mom says
she'll be able to find a job at a restaurant. She says we just need
to get out of here and go someplace with better public transporta-*

tion. It'll be another year before she gets her driver's license back.

I haven't told her yet, but she doesn't have to worry about us ever going hungry. There's tons of free food out there!

It may take me a week to find a computer I can use to write you, but don't worry. I will. Please write soon!

BHD

Next I opened Dinah's e-mail from Thursday.

PK,

Please don't be sad. We'll see each other again someday. I promise. Until then we'll write. Here's the poem I wrote when I spent the night in the barn with the farting cows!

Someone, Anyone

I just want someone to care about me
Someone who'll understand
Someone who wants to listen
Someone to be my friend

Is there anyone who wants to love me?
Anyone who'll let me be
Myself—whoever that is
I only want to be me

Wasn't long before I found you. Thanks for being my some-body.

BHD

I clicked on reply.

BHD,

I hope you like Cincinnati. Mom had a baby girl on Sunday, and they didn't name her Acts. Her name's Katherine Joy, and we call her Katie. She's beautiful. Mom went into labor right in the middle of the morning service. Old Mrs. Miller had her dogs there for the first time, and they went berserk. She's not allowed to bring another dog into the church unless it's really a trained service dog. She'll probably go buy a dozen of them to bring with her while she gets all of her own trained!

I'll write more soon. I miss you!

PK

Next I opened the e-mail from the astrophysicist.

Hello,

Please take a look at this answer for the time dilation formula.

http://imagine.gsfc.nasa.gov/docs/ask_astro/answers/971
109a.html

If you plug in the numbers then you get about .9999993 c
(the speed of light) which is the speed that god must travel to
make the time on earth appear to be 1000x longer.

Hope this helps,
Mike and Georgia for "Ask an Astrophysicist"

I went to the website. It used the same formula I'd
already found and talked about the twin paradox.

In the case of the twin paradox, the assumption is that the
person gets in a ship and then is in this different reference frame.
At some point he turns around, thus switching reference frames
again, and when he gets back home he now is back in the refer-
ence frame of the Earth. Depending on how fast the ship went,
much less time elapsed for him than his twin brother who stayed
at home. This will be shorter by a factor of:

$sqrt(1 - (v/c)^2)$ *: where v = speed and c = speed of light*

If God were traveling at .9999993 times the speed
of light, time on earth would only be going 1000 times
faster. So one year would be like a thousand years. That
couldn't be right. It's supposed to be one *day* is like a

thousand years, not one *year* is like a thousand years. There are 365 days in a year. 365 times a thousand is 365,000. And that's not counting leap year. That's another 250 days. Time on earth should be 365,250 times longer, not just a thousand times longer.

I went back to the web page I found through Jeeves. It went through lots of examples showing that there's not much time dilation at 50% of the speed of light or 75% of the speed of light or even 99% of the speed of light. The real significant time dilation doesn't start until you get to 99.99999% of the speed of light. The NASA astrophysicist only calculated it at 99.99993% of the speed of light. To reach one day is like one thousand years or 365,250 times longer, you have to be going 99.9999999999999% of the speed of light.

Hard to believe that four billionths of a percent could make such a difference. That's like one person out of all the people who have ever lived on the earth. Maybe every little bit can make a big difference in the grand scheme of things. Kind of like a mustard seed.

I copied down all of the calculations and logged off the computer. There was still time for me to sit under our tree and read all of Dinah's poems again. I wondered if the library had any songbooks I could check out with *Blowin' in the Wind* or *What a Wonderful World.* That would be a good project for tomorrow.

About the Author

Laurie Gray earned her B.A. from Goshen College and her J.D. from Indiana University School of Law. Between college and law school, she taught high school Spanish, working summers as an interpreter in Guatemala. An experienced trial attorney and child advocate, Laurie is the founder of Socratic Parenting, LLC (www.SocraticParenting.com). *Summer Sanctuary* is her first novel.